A Cowboy's Second Chance

Riverbend Valley Book 1

Tara Baisden

Sterling Ridge Press LLC

Cover designed by Sterling Ridge Press LLC

Published by: Sterling Ridge Press, LLC www.sterlingridgepress.com

ISBN: 978-1-966093-11-4
Printed in the United States of America

First Edition: March 2025

For permissions, contact: tara@tarabaisden.com or visit www.tarabaisden.com

About The Author

Tara Baisden is a Contemporary Inspirational Romance author who proudly calls the beautiful state of West Virginia her home. Nestled on a sprawling mountainous property, she is surrounded by the peace and serenity of nature. Her days are happily spent in the quiet of country life, writing heartwarming stories of love, faith, and second chances. Tara also enjoys quilting, working in her garden, tending to her beloved pets, and soaking in the beauty of her surroundings.

With deep roots in West Virginia, family is everything to Tara. One of her favorite pastimes is gathering on the front porch with loved ones, sharing stories, laughter, and enjoying the simple, meaningful moments that life offers. When she's not crafting her novels, Tara can often be found exploring the rich history of her home state, visiting local historical sites, and, of course, stopping by every bookstore she passes! Her passion for reading and discovery always fuels her next adventure.

Tara is the author of the Laurel Ridges series of novels, as well as the Riverbend Valley series of novels, of which have been beloved by fans of inspirational romance. Her novels reflect her love for faith, family, and the timeless beauty of the world we live in.

Known for her sweet and clean romances, she creates characters that feel like family and settings that make readers want to visit again and again.

You can find out more about Tara and her latest releases at www.tarabaisden.com or follow her on social media for updates and behind-the-scenes glimpses of her writing process. Stay connected—you won't want to miss the heartfelt stories of love and family she has in store!

Also by Tara Baisden

<u>Riverbend Valley Series</u>

#1 A Cowboy's Second Chance

#2 Wanderlust & Wild Horses

#3 Heartstrings on the Horizon

<u>Laurel Ridge Series</u>

#1. Season of Hope

#2. Finding Grace

#3. His Perfect Plan

#4. Love Redeemed

#5 Snowbound Blessings

#6 Sheltered Hearts

#7 Restoring Faith

#8 Love Rekindled

#9 Where She Belongs

#10 Shelter in His Arms

#11 Where Love Stands

About Riverbend Valley

Welcome to the fictional town of Riverbend Valley, Montana!

Nestled in the shadow of the breathtaking Sapphire Mountains, Riverbend Valley is a place where life flows as peacefully as the rivers winding through it. Surrounded by rolling ranch lands, dense forests, and the rugged peaks of Montana's wilderness, this picturesque valley is the perfect setting for tales of faith, love, and second chances.

A Rugged Heritage

Founded in the late 1800s by homesteaders drawn to the fertile land and expansive views, Riverbend Valley began as a ranching settlement. Riverbend Valley's roots run deep, forged by generations of ranchers and cowboys who've worked the land with grit and determination. This is a place where faith has always been a cornerstone, guiding its people through hardships and celebrating their triumphs. From the well-worn pews of Riverbend Valley Community Church to the lively gatherings at the rodeo grounds, Riverbend Valley's traditions reflect a steadfast commitment to God, family, and the land.

A Community of Faith

Riverbend Valley offers a refuge for weary souls and a chance to redis-cover the beauty of life's simple pleasures. Whether it's through a quiet moment of prayer along the river, a moonlit ride under Montana skies, or the laughter of a community united in celebration, this is a place where hearts are mended, faith is renewed, and love abounds.

The Essence of Small-Town Life

With a population of just over three thousand, Riverbend Valley re-tains its small-town charm. Main Street is lined with family-owned businesses, from the Bluebird Café, famous for its huckleberry pies, to the General Mercantile, where locals gather to swap stories and stock up on supplies. Seasonal festivals bring the community together, from the Spring Rodeo to the Fall Harvest Festival, celebrating the rhythms of life in this ranching town.

A Haven for Visitors

Visitors to Riverbend Valley are captivated by its rustic charm and natural beauty. Whether it's horseback riding through the foothills, fishing in the Deer Run River, or stargazing from Silver Bluff's iconic overlook, there's something for everyone to enjoy.

Experience the Heart of Riverbend Valley

Here, under the endless skies and among the resilient people of Montana, you'll find stories of redemption, second chances, and unwavering faith. Riverbend Valley isn't just a setting—it's a celebration of the rugged heritage and timeless grace that make this place unforgettable. **Welcome to Riverbend Valley, where faith is strong, family is everything, and love always finds a way.**
I hope you fall in love with its enduring spirit.

Dedication

To all those who believe in second chances—
This story is for the hearts that yearn for redemption, the souls that
dare to hope, and the dreamers who trust in love, even when the road
is rocky. May you always find the courage to rewrite your story, the
faith to take one more step, and the grace to embrace the beauty of
new beginnings.
And to my family and friends, whose steadfast love and support remind me every day of God's infinite kindness—you are my greatest
blessing.
With gratitude and love,
Tara

Contents

Chapter 1

Conner Hart gripped the worn steering wheel of his beat-up pickup truck, his knuckles turning white with tension. The tires hummed along the two-lane highway that wound through the endless stretches of Montana's open land. Rolling hills blanketed with lush wild grasses swayed in the evening breeze, and patches of ponderosa pine trees shimmered under the fading light. The towering peaks of the Sapphire Mountains rose in the distance, their snow-capped tips tinged with pink hues from the setting sun.

He hadn't been back to Riverbend Valley in ten long years. A decade since he'd left behind this quiet little town, chasing after glory and fame on the rodeo circuit. A decade since he'd walked away from his father, the Gold Star Ranch, and Rachel Nolan.

The scent of pine wafted through the open window, mingling with the faint aroma of wildflowers that lined the roadside. He inhaled, letting the long forgotten scents wash over him. They stirred something deep within—a mix of nostalgia and regret.

As he approached the familiar welcome sign that read, "Welcome to Riverbend Valley—Where the Mountains Meet the Sky," Conner felt a knot tighten in his stomach. The last time he'd driven this road, he'd been full of youthful arrogance and big dreams. Now, he was returning with little more than a battered duffel bag and a heap of regrets.

He passed by the Deer Run River, its waters glistening under the sunlit sky. Memories flooded his mind—fishing trips with his father, swimming with friends on hot summer days, quiet moments shared with Rachel under the old willow tree by the riverbank. He shook his head, attempting to clear the bittersweet images.

Main Street appeared up ahead, the heart of Riverbend Valley. The storefronts looked much the same, their Western-style facades painted in hues of red, blue, and green. Signs creaked softly in the afternoon breeze, and warm light spilled from the windows, casting a welcoming ambiance onto the sidewalk.

He slowed as he passed the Bluebird Café, the rich aroma of freshly baked breads and brewing coffee wafting out to meet him. Through the large windows, he glimpsed locals seated at tables, chatting and laughing. A pang of longing blindsided him.

The Riverbend Valley Community Church stood proudly at the end of the street, its white steeple reaching skyward. The stained-glass windows reflected the last rays of sunlight, creating a kaleidoscope of colors. Conner felt a flicker of unease.

He continued down the road, passing the Branding Iron Grill. The neon sign buzzed softly, and strains of country music drifted out into the early evening air. Once, he might have stopped in for a drink, but tonight, his destination was clear, and he wasn't in the mood.

Several miles outside of town, he turned onto the long gravel driveway of the Gold Star Ranch. Conner felt his heart rate speed up.

The tires crunched over the stones, and dust kicked up behind him. The sprawling horse pastures stretched out on either side, the wooden fences weathered but sturdy. Silhouettes of horses grazed peacefully, their forms illuminated by the soft glow of the moon now rising in the east.

The main house came into view—a two-story structure with a steep gabled roof and a wide wraparound porch. It stood like a sentinel overlooking the land, just as it had for generations. Conner pulled up and cut the engine, the sudden silence almost deafening.

He sat for a moment, eyes fixed on the house. This was home, yet it felt foreign. A mix of fear and determination welled up inside him.

Stepping out of the truck, he stretched his stiff muscles.

As he approached the porch, the wooden boards creaked beneath his boots—a sound that brought a faint smile to his lips. The porch swing swayed gently in the breeze, chains rattling softly. He remembered sitting there with his mother when he was a young boy, her laughter filling the air as they watched the sunset.

"Well, look who's decided to show up."

Conner turned sharply at the sound of the gruff voice. Standing at the edge of the porch steps was Judd Franklin, the ranch's foreman. Judd was a tall, solidly built man with a square jaw and steel-gray eyes. His weathered face bore the lines of years spent under the sun, and his expression was anything but welcoming.

"Hello, Judd," Conner replied evenly. "It's been a while."

"Not long enough for some," Judd retorted, crossing his arms over his chest. "I wondered if you'd have the courage to come back."

Conner resisted the urge to bristle at the hostility. "I'm here to take care of the ranch. Honor my father's wishes."

Judd snorted, his gaze piercing. "Honor, huh? That's rich coming from you."

He felt the sting of the words but kept his tone measured. "I know I've been gone a long time. But I'm back now and willing to do what's needed."

"Is that so?" Judd's skepticism was palpable. "Folks around here haven't forgotten how you left and never came back, even when your daddy needed you. Neither have I."

"I'm not expecting a warm welcome," Conner admitted. "Just a chance to make things right."

Judd eyed him for a long moment before finally nodding toward the house. "Keys are under the mat. Will and Levi are in the bunkhouse if you need anything. Minnie's gone for the day, but she'll be here tomorrow."

"Thank you," Conner said sincerely.

"Don't thank me yet," Judd replied curtly.

With that, the foreman turned and walked away.

Conner exhaled slowly, the tension easing slightly. The key stuck in the lock, requiring a bit of jiggling before the door finally swung open with a protesting creak. Conner stepped inside, and the musty smell of disuse hit him like a physical force. Dust motes danced in the shafts of sunlight streaming through the windows, and the air was thick with the scent of old leather and memories.

He dropped his bag by the door and moved further into the house, his eyes taking in the familiar surroundings. The foyer led into a spacious living room. He flicked on a light, illuminating the space. The living room looked like a time capsule. The furnishings were much the same: a worn leather sofa, his father's favorite armchair, and the stone fireplace that had warmed many a chilly night. Family photographs adorned the mantel, moments frozen in time.

He stepped closer, picking up a framed picture of himself as a young boy, perched atop a pony, grinning from ear to ear. His father stood beside him, one hand on his shoulder, a rare smile on his usually stern face.

He moved through the house, each room stirring memories. The kitchen, with its checkered curtains and well-worn oak table. The dining room, where countless meals had been shared. The study, where his father spent hours poring over ranch ledgers and correspondence.

Curiosity drew him toward the study. The room was cluttered—papers piled high, books stacked haphazardly, and an array of trinkets collected over the years.

Conner sat in the leather chair behind the desk, running his fingers over the smooth surface. Amidst the mess, a leather-bound journal caught his eye. He pulled it toward him, noting the embossed words on the cover: "Journal: Warren Hart."

He hesitated, fingers hovering over the cover. After a moment, he opened it, flipping through the pages filled with entries dating back several years.

"Started repairing the south fence today. Can't believe how fast time flies. Feels like just yesterday, Conner was helping me mend that very same fence..."

Conner swallowed hard, emotions swirling within him. He continued reading, finding entries that spoke of remorse, longing, and an unmistakable shift in his father's tone.

"Rachel stopped by today. Brought some cookies she baked. She sat with me for a while, talking about forgiveness and faith. It's been years since I stepped foot in a church, but maybe it's time..."

Conner's eyes widened. His father? In church?

"Attended service this morning with Rachel. Felt strange at first, but Pastor Sam's words hit me hard, and I listened and took it all to heart. Maybe there's a chance that I'll make it to heaven. Even an old fool like me is forgiven."

He leaned back, processing the revelation. His father had found faith. And Rachel had been there with him.

***

Conner opened the fridge, only to be met with emptiness and the faint smell of something long past its expiration date. He slammed the door shut, frustration bubbling up inside him. He should have thought about food on the way through town earlier.

"Guess I need to make a supply run," he muttered, running a hand through his hair.

The idea of going into town made Conner's palms sweat, but he knew he couldn't avoid it forever. Might as well rip off the Band-Aid now. He grabbed his keys and headed back out to his truck.

The drive into town was short, but felt like an eternity. As Conner parked in front of the Valley Grocery Store, he could feel curious eyes on him. He took a deep breath, steeling himself before stepping out of the truck.

As he entered, the hum of conversation died down. Conner kept his head down, grabbing a basket and making his way through the aisles. He could hear whispers following him, could practically feel the judgment radiating off the other shoppers.

"Well, if it isn't Conner Hart," a voice called out. Conner looked up to see Kathryn Gillman behind the counter, her gray hair pulled back in a bun. Her eyes, once warm and welcoming, now held a hint of wariness. "I wondered when we'd see you again. It's been awhile."

Conner shifted uncomfortably. "It has. Came back to take care of the ranch, Mrs. Gillman."

Kathryn's lips pressed into a thin line. "Mmm-hmm. Well, I wish you luck. Your daddy left you something good—God rest his soul. You know, he was a changed man these past few years, Conner. I'm sorry you missed that."

The words hit Conner like a physical blow. He nodded, unable to meet her eyes, and turned back to his shopping. He grabbed the essentials—bread, milk, coffee—trying to ignore the stares.

As he reached for a can of beans, a flash of honey blonde hair caught his eye. Conner's heart lurched as he recognized the figure at the end of the aisle. Rachel Nolan stood there, her hazel eyes wide with surprise and something else—pain, maybe, or anger. Probably both.

"Rachel," Conner breathed, his voice barely above a whisper. Her name on his lips felt heavy.

She stiffened, her grip tightening on the basket in her hands. "Conner."

He took a step towards her. His gaze stayed locked on hers, words tumbling out before he could stop them. "Rachel, I... it's good to see you."

Her eyes flashed, and for a moment, Conner thought he saw a flicker of the old Rachel. But it was quickly replaced by an icy mask. "Wish I could say the same."

Before Conner could respond, Rachel brushed past him, the scent of her perfume—still the same after all these years—lingering in the air. He watched her walk away, feeling like he'd been punched in the gut.

Chapter 2

Rachel tightened her grip on the paper grocery bag as she pushed open the wooden gate that led to the front porch of the Nolan farmhouse. Balancing the bag against her hip, Rachel climbed the steps and nudged the front door open with her shoulder.

"Anybody home?" she called out, her voice echoing in the cozy entryway.

"In the kitchen!" Felicia's cheerful reply floated back.

Rachel kicked off her boots and lined them up beside Missy's on the worn rug. She could hear the soft sound of a country song playing on the radio and the clatter of dishes being set on the table. Taking a deep breath, she willed herself to shake off the lingering tension.

Entering the open-concept kitchen and living area, Rachel found Felicia stirring a pot on the stove, her dark hair pulled back into a loose braid. Missy sat at the large oak table, flipping through a magazine while sipping iced tea.

"We were wondering when you'd get home," Missy teased without looking up. "We were starting to think you'd got lost or something."

Rachel forced a smile. "Lost track of time. The line at the store was longer than usual."

Felicia gave her a knowing glance. "You mean Kathryn talked your ear off again?"

"Not exactly." Rachel set the grocery bag on the counter and began unpacking the contents—apples, a loaf of bread, a block of cheddar cheese.

Missy looked up, her sharp blue eyes narrowing. "You okay? You seem... tense."

"I'm fine," Rachel replied a bit too quickly. She could feel both sisters' eyes on her as she reached for a knife to slice the bread.

"Uh-huh." Missy exchanged a glance with Felicia. "You slamming cupboards isn't like you, sis. What's got you all riled up?"

Rachel hadn't realized she'd been closing the cupboard doors with a bit more force than necessary. She sighed, setting the knife down. "It's nothing. Really."

Felicia wiped her hands on a towel and leaned against the counter. "Come on, Rachel. We know you better than that. Did something happen at the store?"

Rachel hesitated. "I ran into someone."

Missy's eyebrows arched. "Someone?"

Rachel met her gaze. "Conner's back."

Felicia's expression softened, but Missy's eyes flashed with irritation.

"Well, isn't that just the cherry on top of a sundae?" Missy scoffed. "That man has some nerve showing his face after all this time."

"Missy," Felicia chided gently. "Let's hear what Rachel has to say."

"What is there to say?" Rachel shrugged, feigning nonchalance. "His daddy died and left him the ranch. I should have expected he'd come back. I saw him at the store. We exchanged a few words. End of story."

Felicia studied her sister closely. "How did he seem?"

Rachel paused, searching for the right words. "Different. Older. But still the same in some ways." She shook her head. "I don't know. The whole thing just caught me off guard."

"I bet." Missy folded her arms. "So what does he want?"

"I really didn't give him much of a chance to talk. I kept it short and walked away," Rachel said.

"I imagine he's here to sell the ranch to the first interested person without a second thought and walk away with millions. That's precisely what someone like him would do. He's a snake."

"Missy!" Felicia's tone was sharp. "That's uncalled for."

Rachel closed her eyes briefly, the image of Conner's face in the grocery store flashing in her mind. The mix of surprise and regret in his eyes had unsettled her more than she'd cared to admit.

"Look," Rachel said, her voice steadier than she felt. "It's none of our concern. I've moved on. We'll have to see each other on the ranch while he's here. That's it."

Felicia reached out to touch Rachel's arm. "Are you sure you're okay with that?"

"I have to be," Rachel replied, pulling away gently. "The ranch means too much to me to let personal history get in the way. I enjoy my job there."

Missy snorted. "Just don't let him worm his way back in, Rachel. People like that don't change."

Felicia shot her a warning look. "Everyone deserves a second chance, Missy. You know that."

"Maybe some people do, but not him." Missy stood up. "I'm going to check on the laundry."

Felicia turned back to Rachel, her eyes full of concern.

"You know she just wants to protect you," Felicia said softly.

"I know." Rachel managed a small smile. "She wears her heart on her sleeve."

Felicia laughed lightly. "That's one way to put it." She paused, then added, "But how do you really feel about Conner being back?"

Rachel took a deep breath, her gaze drifting to the kitchen window. The sun was dipping low on the horizon, casting hues of pink and orange over the rolling hills. "I don't know," she admitted. "Part of me wants to pretend he doesn't exist. Another part..." she trailed off.

"Another part still cares?" Felicia finished gently.

Rachel swallowed hard. "It's been ten years, Felicia. People change. I've changed. I'm not that naïve girl anymore."

"No, you're not. You're a strong, independent woman who's built a good life for herself."

"Exactly." Rachel nodded firmly. "And I won't let anyone disrupt that."

Felicia studied her for a moment before speaking. "Just remember, guarding your heart doesn't mean shutting it down completely."

Rachel looked at her sister, seeing the worry etched on her gentle features. "I appreciate your concern, but I'm fine. Really."

"If you say so." Felicia reached over and squeezed Rachel's hand. "Just know I'm here if you need to talk."

"Thanks." Rachel squeezed back, grateful for her sister's unwavering support.

The truth was, seeing Conner had shaken her more than she cared to admit. The years had been kind to him, adding a ruggedness to his features that hadn't been there before. But it was the look in his eyes—a mix of sorrow and something she couldn't quite identify—that nagged at her.

She busied herself ladling stew into bowls as Missy returned, her expression softer.

"Smells so good," Missy commented, taking her seat at the table.

"It does," Rachel replied, passing around the basket of bread.

They bowed their heads as Felicia offered grace. "Lord, we thank You for this meal and for bringing us together tonight. Please bless our family and guide us through whatever challenges lie ahead. Amen."

"Amen," the sisters echoed.

They ate in relative silence, the only sounds the clink of spoons against bowls and the occasional sigh. Finally, Missy couldn't hold back any longer.

"So, what do you think the plans are for the ranch now that Conner's back?" she asked, looking pointedly at Rachel.

Rachel suppressed a sigh. "I honestly have no idea. I plan to just keep doing my job. I'm not going to worry over anything until there is a reason to worry."

"You'll see him every day," Missy said.

"I can handle it," Rachel said firmly.

"Can you?" Missy raised an eyebrow.

Felicia intervened. "Let's not assume the worst. Maybe this is an opportunity for healing."

Rachel set her spoon down, her appetite gone. "I appreciate your concern, both of you, but I'm a grown woman. I can take care of myself."

Missy held up her hands defensively. "Alright, alright. I'll drop it."

An awkward silence followed. Rachel pushed her bowl away and stood up. "I'm going to go check on the horses before it gets too dark."

Felicia glanced out the window. "It looks like a storm might be rolling in."

"I'll be fine." Rachel grabbed her denim jacket from the hook by the door. "Don't wait up."

She stepped out onto the back porch, the evening air cool against her skin. Dark clouds were gathering on the horizon, but there was still enough light to make it to the stables.

As she approached the barn, the soft nickering of horses greeted her.

"Hey there," she murmured, running a hand down the muzzle of a chestnut mare named Ginger. "How's my girl?"

Ginger nuzzled her hand, searching for treats. Rachel smiled and pulled a sugar cube from her pocket.

"Don't tell the others," she whispered conspiratorially.

She moved down the row, checking on each horse, the routine soothing her restless mind. Being here, among the animals she cared for, always brought her peace.

But tonight, even the tranquility of the stables couldn't chase away the thoughts swirling in her head. Leaning against the stall door, Rachel closed her eyes.

"Why now?" she whispered to the empty barn. "Why bring him back into my life after all this time?"

The only response was the soft rustling of hay and the distant rumble of thunder.

"Mom always said God doesn't give us more than we can handle," she mused aloud. "But sometimes I wonder."

Trusting Conner again seemed impossible after everything he'd put her through. He had walked away without a single word, pursuing a life that cast her aside like a forgotten promise. How could she open her heart to someone who had abandoned her so effortlessly, chasing after ambitions that excluded her entirely?

She shook her head firmly, willing the painful thoughts to subside. There were more pressing matters at hand—the Gold Star Ranch required her dedication, the horses there relied on her care, she'd made a promise to Warren Hart before he died to stay on at the ranch and keep training the horses, and she refused to let Conner's sudden return disrupt the life she had painstakingly built that didn't revolve around him anymore.

Chapter 3

C onner stood outside the ranch office, his gaze fixed on the weathered wooden door that had welcomed and dismissed countless visitors over the years.

Sunlight streamed through the large paned windows, casting dancing patterns on the polished wooden floor as he opened the office door. The interior was a comforting mix of the old and the timeless—wooden beams crossing the ceiling, walls adorned with photographs of prized horses and ranch events, and shelves lined with well-worn ledgers and books.

"Conner Hart, as I live and breathe!"

He looked over to see Minnie Montgomery rising from behind her cluttered desk. Her silver-streaked hair was neatly pinned back, and her eyes sparkled behind wire-rimmed glasses. She moved toward him with surprising agility, arms open wide.

"Minnie," Conner replied, a genuine smile spreading across his face. He accepted her embrace, the warmth and familiarity easing some of the tension knotting his stomach.

"Let me get a good look at you," she said, holding him at arm's length. "Still as handsome as ever, though perhaps a bit more rough around the edges."

"Time does that to a person," he said.

She chuckled. "Well, it certainly hasn't dampened your charm." Gesturing toward a chair, she added, "Judd left me a note on my desk and said you were back. I expected to see you eventually. Come, sit. We've got plenty to catch up on."

Conner settled into the chair opposite her desk, taking in the organized chaos of her workspace—stacks of papers, a collection of mismatched mugs holding pens and pencils, and a calendar adorned with pictures of serene landscapes.

"Place looks just the same," he remarked, noting the familiar items, a ceramic horse figurine on the windowsill, the old cuckoo clock ticking softly on the wall, and a faded poster promoting the county fair from years past.

"Why fix what isn't broken?" Minnie replied, easing back into her chair. "Besides, I like to think of it as a vintage vibe."

He grinned. "Fair enough."

She leaned forward, her expression turning earnest. "I'm glad you're here, Conner. Truly."

"Thank you," he said. "I know it's been a long time."

"Water under the bridge." She waved a hand dismissively. "What's important is that you're back."

He nodded, though a part of him wondered if it would be that simple with everyone else.

"Well now," she said, pulling a hefty ledger toward her. "I figure you're eager to get up to speed on the ranch's operations first. But you have to promise me—you'll let me in on everything that's happened with you these past ten years. I did my best to follow your rodeo career.

When I heard about your injury, my heart sank. I hoped and prayed you'd find a way to keep going... but I suppose the good Lord had different plans in mind for you."

Conner inhaled deeply, the memories stirring within him. "Yeah, He certainly did. Let's focus on the ranch for now, though. Once I've got a handle on things, I'd love to take you out to dinner and catch up properly." He offered a reassuring smile. "Right now, I need to get up to speed. Tell me everything—how the ranch has been running, our financial situation, any obstacles we're dealing with. I want to understand where we stand so I can help."

"Diving right in. Your father would be proud," she said with a smile.

Conner's gaze dropped momentarily. "I hope so."

Minnie opened the ledger, flipping to a marked page. "Let's start with the financials. Overall, the ranch is stable—for now. But as you can see here," she pointed to a column of numbers, "our profits have been declining steadily over the past few years."

He studied the figures, his brow furrowing. "Feed costs have increased significantly."

"Yes, and the market prices for horses have been unpredictable," she added. "We've had to dip into reserves more than once."

"What about our revenue streams? Any new buyers or contracts?"

"We've maintained relationships with our regular buyers, but competition has been stiff. Several new ranches have cropped up, offering lower prices. It's been challenging to stay competitive without cutting into our margins."

Conner leaned back, considering. "Have we explored diversifying? Offering services beyond our traditional operations?"

Minnie gave a thoughtful nod. "It's been discussed, but your father was... hesitant to make changes. Please understand, he really had some trying health issues these last few years."

"I'm not my father," he said gently. "I think it's time we consider new avenues. For instance, we could entice some of the visitors that come to vacation in the area. We could offer trail rides, or even open up parts of the ranch for guest stays. We could even host training clinics for the locals in the area."

She smiled slightly. "I always knew you had a head for business. Those ideas have merit, though we'd need to assess the costs and logistics."

"Agreed," he replied. "I'll work on some proposals and some more ideas. But I value your input—and that of the staff."

"We'll figure it out together," Minnie patted his hand and continued, "You were always so creative and had such a head for this business. I'm so glad you're back, Conner.

He glanced around the office once more, his eyes landing on a framed photograph of his father and Rachel standing beside a magnificent stallion. They both looked so at ease, so connected to the ranch and to each other. A pang of regret pierced him.

"She was a great help to your father, especially in his later years," Minnie said softly, following his gaze.

"Rachel?" he asked, though he already knew the answer.

"Yes. She was like family to him. They shared a deep bond over the horses. Rachel still works here on the ranch... she's an excellent trainer."

Conner swallowed. "I regret not being here. Minnie, I honestly didn't know dad was sick. When I got the news that he had passed, I was shocked."

Minnie squeezed his hand. "You're here now, and that's what matters."

Just then, the office door swung open.

"Minnie, about the supply order for next week—"

Rachel stopped abruptly upon seeing Conner, her hazel eyes widening before narrowing slightly. She stood in the doorway, her posture stiff, a folder clutched to her chest.

"Rachel," Minnie exclaimed, a hint of amusement in her tone. "Perfect timing. Conner and I were just discussing some new ideas for the ranch. Perhaps you could join us?"

Rachel's gaze flickered between them. "I didn't realize there was a meeting."

"More of an impromptu discussion," Conner said, rising to his feet. "Good morning, Rachel."

"Conner," she acknowledged coolly. "I don't want to interrupt. I can come back later."

"Nonsense," Minnie declared, standing up. "Actually, I need to check on something in the storeroom. Why don't you two continue?"

Before either could protest, she swept past Rachel, offering them both a cheerful smile as she exited.

An awkward silence enveloped the room. Conner gestured toward the chair Minnie had vacated. "Would you like to sit?"

Rachel shook her head. "I'm fine standing."

He nodded, slipping his hands into his pockets. "Minnie was just going over the ranch's financials with me. I'm trying to get a handle on things so I can keep the ranch running smoothly."

"Financials are Minnie's domain," she replied evenly.

"Yes, but I thought it might be helpful to get caught up on where we stand financially. Now, I'd like to get your perspective, especially on the horse training operations."

She raised an eyebrow. "My perspective?"

"Yes. Minnie mentioned you've been doing exceptional work with the horses. I was thinking we could explore ways to expand that side of the business, could increase revenue."

Rachel regarded him skeptically. "Such as?"

He stepped closer, his enthusiasm growing. "Well, perhaps we could host training clinics, offer specialized lessons, or even breed for specific markets."

She crossed her arms. "That's a lot of change."

"I know. But I believe it could bring in additional revenue and secure the ranch's future."

"Secure the ranch's future," she repeated, a hint of sarcasm in her tone. "And what makes you think you know what's best for the ranch?"

He paused, taken aback. "I don't know what's best for the ranch at all. But the ranch is my concern now, and I want to see it succeed. I'm here to help."

"Help," she echoed. "After ten years of silence, you suddenly want to help."

Conner felt a flush rise to his cheeks. "I deserve that remark, Rachel. But I'm here now, and I'm committed to making things right."

"Committed," she said, her eyes flashing. "You were committed once before. How did that turn out?"

He took a deep breath, fighting to keep his voice steady. "I can't change the past, Rachel. I did what I did. But I'm going to try to make amends."

She held his gaze for a long moment before shaking her head. "I have work to do."

"Rachel, please," he implored.

"I'll continue to do my job here. I promised your father I would," she replied curtly. "Whether or not you're here doesn't change that."

With that, she turned on her heel and walked out, leaving the door ajar.

Conner exhaled slowly, a mix of frustration and regret swirling within him. He sank back into the chair, running a hand through his hair.

"Well, that went well," he muttered.

"Don't take it personally," came Minnie's voice from the doorway.

He looked up to see her re-entering, a sympathetic expression on her face.

"She has every right to be upset," Conner said.

"Yes, she does. But time has a way of healing," Minnie offered gently. "Just give it some time."

He sighed. "I hope you're right."

She settled back at her desk. "Give her space. Focus on the tasks at hand. The rest will follow."

"Speaking of tasks," he said, eager to shift the conversation, "I think I'll start by helping with some of the maintenance around here. I'm going to sit down with Judd later this afternoon and get more of a handle on what needs attention."

"That's a good idea," she agreed. "Getting your hands dirty might remind everyone, including yourself, that you're serious about being here."

He stood. "Then I'd better get to it."

Minnie smiled. "Keep your chin up, Conner. Things will work out just the way they're meant to."

Chapter 4

Conner adjusted his Stetson as he stepped out of the ranch office, shielding his eyes from the early light as he surveyed the expanse before him. Horses grazed lazily in the pastures, their coats gleaming in the sunlight.

As he rounded the corner of the barn, he caught sight of Judd leaning casually against the fence bordering the north arena. Judd's weathered hat was pulled low over his brow, arms resting on the top rail as he watched something intently. Conner followed his gaze and felt his heart skip a beat.

Rachel was in the arena, working with a spirited chestnut mare. The horse tossed its head, mane flying as it pranced nervously. Rachel's posture was relaxed yet commanding, one hand gripping the reins loosely, while the other held a training whip she used more as a guide than a threat. Her blonde hair was pulled back into a loose braid that cascaded over her shoulder, and even from a distance, Conner could see the determined set of her jaw.

He hesitated for a moment, torn between the urge to watch her and the need to speak with Judd. Shaking off the distraction, he approached the fence.

"Mind if I join you?" Conner asked, keeping his tone neutral.

Judd glanced at him briefly, his expression unreadable beneath the brim of his hat. "Free country."

Conner rested his arms on the fence rail, mimicking Judd's posture. For a few moments, they stood in silence, watching Rachel guide the mare through a series of exercises. The horse responded to her every cue, gradually calming under her gentle command.

"She's good with them," Conner said.

"Always has been," Judd replied tersely.

Conner stole another glance at Rachel. The way she moved, the subtle gestures, the soft words he couldn't quite make out, all of it spoke to a deep connection with the animal. It was as if they communicated on a level beyond simple commands.

"I wanted to talk to you," Conner began, turning his attention back to Judd. "Think we could chat for a minute?"

Judd straightened up, fixing Conner with a hard stare. "Depends on what you've got to say."

Conner met his gaze steadily. "I know you and I haven't exactly seen eye to eye in the past, but I want to make things right. I'm here to work, and run this ranch, and I need to get up to speed on what needs doing around the ranch."

Judd raised an eyebrow. "You're suddenly interested in ranch work again? Your daddy dies, and you come waltzing back here like nothing's changed. Thought your talents were elsewhere."

Conner resisted the urge to bristle. "I've always been interested in the ranch, just took me a while to realize where I belonged. And to grow up a bit."

"Hmm." Judd turned back to watch Rachel, who was now leading the mare around the arena at a steady trot. "So, what is it you want from me?"

"I'd like you to catch me up on your duties. Tell me what's been happening around here, what's priority. I want to keep things running smoothly."

Judd was silent for a moment, eyes fixed on the horse and rider. "And you expect me to believe you're sticking around this time?"

Conner took a deep breath. "Yes. I'm committed to being here, to doing what's right by this ranch and my father. Look, we need to start over on the right foot."

"Words are easy, Conner." Judd glanced at him again. "You've got a long way to go to prove that to anyone around here."

"I understand that," Conner said evenly. "But everyone has to start somewhere."

"Suppose that's true." Judd sighed, adjusting his hat. "All right. Fence along the south pasture needs mending. The horses have been testing it, and the last thing we need is a herd wandering off."

Conner nodded. "I can handle that. What else?"

"Roof on the equipment shed has a leak. Been meaning to patch it up. And the corral gate's sticking—we've oiled it, but it might need new hinges."

"Got it." Conner reached into his pocket and pulled out a small notebook, jotting down the tasks. "Anything else?"

"Well, since you're asking, the tractor's been acting up. Might need a look over. Not sure if you're any good with engines, though."

"I can manage," Conner replied, a hint of a smile tugging at his lips. "Used to work on them with Dad."

Judd grunted in acknowledgment.

From the corner of his eye, Conner saw Rachel transition the mare into a canter, the horse's movements fluid and graceful. He couldn't help but admire the synergy between them. Rachel sat tall in the saddle, exuding confidence and calm.

"She's planning to enter Luna in the county show," Judd commented, following Conner's gaze.

"Luna?" Conner asked.

"The mare," Judd clarified. "Skittish thing when she got here. Rachel's been working wonders with her."

"She's always had a gift," Conner said.

"That she has." Judd turned to face him fully. "Look, Conner, I don't know what your intentions are, but if you're thinking of stirring up old dust with Rachel, you'd best think twice."

Conner met his stare. "I don't plan on causing her any more pain. I just want to make things right."

"Making things right, huh?" Judd's voice held a note of skepticism. "And what does that mean, exactly?"

"It means owning up to my mistakes," Conner said firmly. "I know I hurt her. I can't change the past, but I'm hoping in time..." He trailed off, unsure how to articulate the jumble of emotions swirling inside him.

Judd's eyes narrowed. "Rachel's been through enough. She doesn't need you waltzing back in and turning her world upside down."

"I'm not here to make things harder for her," Conner insisted. "I just want a chance to make amends for everything I did wrong in the past and to prove I've changed."

"Changed, have you?" Judd's tone was flat.

"Yes," Conner replied, steel edging into his voice.

Judd studied him for a long moment before nodding slowly. "We'll see."

They lapsed into silence again, the sounds of the ranch filling the void. Rachel brought Luna to a halt in the center of the arena, patting the mare's neck and speaking soothing words that carried faintly on the breeze.

"She's entering the county show, you said?" Conner asked.

"That's right. Could be good for the ranch. If Luna performs well, it might draw some positive attention."

"Do you think she stands a chance?"

Judd shrugged. "Horse has the talent, and Rachel's got the skill. Just depends on whether they can overcome a few hurdles."

Conner tilted his head. "What kind of hurdles?"

"Trust issues. Luna spooks easily. Rachel's been working on it, but it's touch and go."

Conner considered this. "Maybe I could help."

Judd barked a laugh. "And how do you figure you'd do that?"

"I've dealt with tough horses before," Conner said. "Maybe an extra hand wouldn't hurt."

Judd's expression hardened again. "I think Rachel has it under control."

"It's just an offer," Conner replied, holding up his hands. "I'm not trying to step on any toes."

"Best to let her be," Judd said tersely. "She doesn't need you or any distractions."

Conner pressed his lips together, choosing not to argue. "Fine. I'll focus on the repairs."

"Good idea." Judd pushed away from the fence. "I've got work to do. If you need supplies, check the shed behind the barn. Should have everything you need."

"Thanks," Conner said. "And Judd, whether or not you like it, I'm here to stay. This chip you have on your shoulder needs to stop. Maybe try to remember who's signing your paychecks now."

As Judd walked away, Conner remained at the fence, eyes drifting back to Rachel. She had dismounted and was leading Luna out of the arena, pausing occasionally to let the mare graze on patches of clover. The sunlight caught her hair, creating a halo effect that made Conner's chest tighten.

Chapter 5

Conner stood on the sidewalk of Main Street, his gaze fixed on the red-brick building that housed Joel Ellison's law office. The bustling sounds of Riverbend Valley faded into the background as he took a deep breath.

Conner squared his shoulders and pushed open the heavy oak door. The reception area was exactly as he remembered—warm and inviting. Red oak wooden floors creaked under his boots as he stepped inside, and the ticking of a grandfather clock filled the quiet space.

"Well, if it isn't Conner Hart," a cheerful voice called out.

He turned to see Lillian Barstowe, the ever-smiling secretary, seated behind a polished mahogany desk. Her dark hair was pulled into a neat bun, and her eyes crinkled at the corners as she grinned.

"Good to see you again, Lillian," Conner replied, forcing a smile. "It's been a while."

"Too long. My haven't you turned into a handsome man. I'm sorry for your loss. Your daddy was a good man," she said, tapping a perfectly manicured nail on the desk.

"Thanks, Lillian. I wish I would have been here for him when he needed me."

"Well, you're here now. Joel's expecting you. Go right on in, sugar," she said.

"Thanks." He nodded before he moved toward the office door.

Conner knocked lightly before turning the brass handle. Pushing the door open, he stepped into Joel's office and froze.

Sitting across from the large oak desk was Rachel.

Her hair was loose and flowing. She wore a crisp white blouse tucked into dark denim jeans. She glanced up, her hazel eyes widening in surprise before narrowing with a guarded expression.

"Rachel…" Conner's voice trailed off. "I didn't expect to see you here."

"Clearly," she replied coolly, her gaze flickering away.

Joel Ellison, a stout man with silver-streaked hair and kind eyes, stood up from behind his neat desk. "Conner! Good to see you made it." He extended a hand.

Conner tore his eyes away from Rachel and shook Joel's hand firmly. "Joel. What's going on? Why is Rachel here?"

Joel gestured to the empty chair beside Rachel. "Please, have a seat. We have some important matters to discuss, and it's best if you're both here."

Conner hesitated before settling into the chair, acutely aware of Rachel's presence beside him. The scent of her perfume, a favorite of his, tugged at memories he'd tried to bury.

"Look, I apologize for the surprise," Joel began, smoothing out a stack of papers. "But I thought it was important you both hear this together."

Rachel crossed her arms, her posture stiff. "You could have given us a heads-up, Joel."

Joel offered a sympathetic smile. "Perhaps, but sometimes it's better to address things head-on without preconceived notions getting in the way."

Conner suppressed a sigh. "What's this all about, Joel?"

Joel adjusted his glasses and took a seat. "It's about your father's will."

Conner felt a tightening in his chest at the mention of his father. Warren Hart hadn't been an easy man to love, but news of his death had hit Conner hard. Regrets and unresolved feelings swirled within him, but he pushed them aside. "And with Rachel being here, I assume that means she's in the will as well. Let's get on with it then."

Joel nodded. "Very well." He picked up a thick envelope, extracting several documents. "Your father left specific instructions regarding the Gold Star Ranch, and both of you are directly involved."

Conner cast a sidelong glance at Rachel. She stared straight ahead, her jaw set.

"Conner," Joel continued, "your father has stipulated that in order for you to inherit the Gold Star Ranch, you must live and work on the ranch for one full year. During this time, you are to manage the operations, learn the ins and outs, and show a commitment to its success. Once a month, you need to stop in and see me and give me updates on how everything is going."

Conner blinked, absorbing the information. "A year? Makes sense. I intend to stay regardless."

Joel met his gaze steadily. "There's more. He wants you to embrace and expand on the legacy he built."

"Of course." Conner rubbed a hand over his face. "But out of curiosity, what if I don't?"

"If you fail to meet the conditions of the will," Joel said slowly, "ownership of the ranch will transfer to Rachel Nolan."

Conner's head snapped up. "Wait, what? Rachel inherits if I don't comply?"

Rachel shifted uncomfortably, but remained silent.

"That's correct," Joel affirmed. "Additionally, Rachel, your employment at the ranch is guaranteed for the next two years. You cannot be dismissed during this period for any reason unless I deem it necessary."

Conner felt a surge of frustration. "So we're both literally stuck. And we have to work together."

Joel leaned forward, his expression earnest. "Your father believed this arrangement would be beneficial—for you, for Rachel, and for the ranch. He wanted to ensure its future was in capable hands."

Conner clenched his jaw. "He always did like pulling the strings."

Rachel finally spoke, her voice steady but edged with tension. "He mentioned making provisions for the ranch, but I didn't know he'd go this far. He kept the details to himself."

Conner glanced at her, noting the way her eyes flashed with a mix of emotions he couldn't quite decipher. "You didn't know about any of this?"

She met his gaze unflinchingly. "I had an inkling he was planning something, but I didn't expect this."

Silence settled over the room, heavy and suffocating.

Joel cleared his throat. "I understand this is a lot to take in. But I trust you'll both honor Warren's wishes. The ranch's future depends on it."

Conner stood abruptly, the chair scraping against the wooden floor. "Is that all?"

"Well," Joel continued, "your dad also requests that you not interfere with Rachel's job and vice versa. Rachel, you are to focus on your work and not interfere with or question the way Conner runs the ranch. Conner, the same goes for you. Your dad specifically states that Rachel is in charge of all training for the horses on the ranch, and she doesn't need to seek your permission for her training methods. You both are to have a monthly meeting with Minnie Montgomery and update her on everything going on at the ranch in your individual departments, and she will inform you both of the overall financial health of the ranch. Minnie, in turn, will create a document each month on how you both are doing and the work you've done on the ranch, the financials, etc., and email it to me. And of course, if you can both work out your differences and work together, I can decide if we can forego the monthly meetings with Minnie."

"Okay, so you basically will oversee everything and make sure we are doing what we are supposed to be doing. What else?" Conner said, as he sat back down.

"There's a clause in the will that guarantees Minnie Montgomery can keep her job on the ranch for as long as she wishes," he continued. "If any issues arise concerning her employment, come to me, and I'll handle it."

"That makes sense," Conner replied. "Minnie has always done a fantastic job. Anything else?"

"Your dad was well covered under his life insurance policy," Joel began gently. "I've taken care of all the funeral home expenses and ensured all his medical bills have been paid in full. The remaining funds from the policy are designated to purchase new horses for the ranch, to be trained by Rachel. She is to select and purchase them as she sees fit. Additionally, your father chose to be cremated, Conner. His last wishes were to have no formal funeral, just a simple graveside ceremony with Pastor Sam officiating. Warren requested that you personally, Conner, bury him in the family cemetery at Gold Star Ranch.

His remains are currently at the funeral home, waiting for you to collect."

Conner shifted uncomfortably in his seat, running a hand through his hair. "Joel, this is... a lot. I haven't dealt with death since my mom passed, and that was years ago. I was only eight. I was just a kid then. This all feels so final. So forgive me if I seem... lost. What exactly do I need to do?"

"You pick up your dad's ashes," Rachel interjected, her tone sharp. "You dig his grave in the cemetery, and you lay him to rest after Pastor Sam says a few words. If you have any decency left, you'll say a prayer over him and let him rest in peace. Might not hurt to pray for forgiveness for yourself. For not being here when your daddy needed you most, Conner."

Her words struck Conner like a physical blow, stealing the breath from his lungs. He hadn't expected such bitterness. Rachel had grown more outspoken in the ten years he'd been away.

"Rachel, take it down a notch," Conner said as he glanced at her. "I know you're upset with me, but let's try to be civil, okay?"

Rachel ignored him.

"Conner, I understand this is overwhelming," Joel said. "Dealing with a death is never easy, especially when it's sudden. I know it's a shock. I'm here to assist you if you'd like, but your father was adamant that you be the one to bury him."

Conner took a deep breath, nodding slowly. "I understand. I'll handle it. I just... assumed he was already laid to rest. But I'll take care of it." He glanced between Joel and Rachel. "Is there anything else in the will we should know about, Joel?"

"Your dad left you a sizeable sum of money, Conner," Joel said, his voice gentle yet firm. He shuffled some papers on his desk before meeting Conner's eyes. "I can help you with the details whenever you're ready." Turning slightly, he addressed Rachel. "Rachel, you also have a significant amount in an account that Warren set up for you. There are no stipulations attached to either of your inheritances. Warren simply wanted to ensure you both were provided for, and he's also made a generous contribution to the Gold Star Ranch bank account. These funds should be released soon, so you both have access to the accounts. The transfer of funds to the Gold Star's account should take place next week."

Conner felt a mix of surprise and confusion swirling within him. He glanced over at Rachel, noticing the way her fingers clenched tightly in her lap. "I get the feeling you made quite an impression on my dad," he drawled. "He's made sure the ranch and both of us are looked after. Care to enlighten me on what happened in the past ten years?"

Rachel's gaze snapped up to meet his, her hazel eyes flashing with a blend of hurt and defiance. She took a deep breath, and for a moment, he saw a flicker of vulnerability before she masked it. Looking away, she fixed her stare on a framed photograph on the wall. "I was here for him, Conner," she said, her voice steady but edged with emotion. "I was here when he quit drinking. I stood beside him through every struggle, every temptation. I was here when he was diagnosed with liver failure. I helped him navigate the doctors, the treatments. I prayed for him, introduced him to God when he was searching for something to hold on to. I took him to church, sat with him in the pew when he felt out of place. I answered his questions, no matter how tough they were. I was there for him in the end."

She paused, her voice catching slightly. "Conner, I held his hand as he took his last breath. So don't question why I'm included in the will. Your dad and I grew close these past ten years after you abandoned us both. Whether or not you accept it, he became a different man—a better man. You just weren't around to see any of it."

Conner didn't know what to say. He stared at Rachel at a loss for words.

"For now," Joel continued. "There are papers to sign, but do either of you have questions?"

As Joel laid the documents before them, Rachel and Conner both shook their heads in silent acknowledgment. Rachel picked up the pen, glanced over the papers, and signed her name. Conner watched her intently before speaking. "I really am sorry, Rachel. I had no idea. Thank you for being there for Dad."

She met his gaze. "You're welcome."

Standing up, Rachel smoothed her blouse. "Thank you, Joel," she said.

Conner signed the papers next, then rose and shook Joel's hand.

As they turned to leave, Joel called after them. "My door is always open if either of you have questions—or if you just want to talk."

"Appreciate it," Conner muttered.

In the reception area, the grandfather clock chimed, marking the passing hour. Conner hesitated, feeling the weight of the situation pressing down on him. Rachel was a step ahead, her footsteps light on the polished floor.

"Rachel."

She paused, and turned to face him, eyes wary. "What?"

"About all this... I'm sorry you got dragged into it."

She raised an eyebrow. "Dragged into it? Conner, I've been part of the ranch for years. Your father entrusted me with its care. This isn't just about you."

He bristled at her tone, but knew she was right. "I didn't mean it that way. It's just—"

"Just what?" she challenged.

He sighed, searching for the right words. "I know things between us are... complicated. But I want you to know I plan on fulfilling the terms. I will not walk away again."

Her expression softened ever so slightly before hardening again. "We'll see."

With that, she exited the office.

Conner stood there for a moment, staring after her. The ache of regret settled in his chest.

"Everything okay, dear?" Lillian's voice cut through his thoughts.

He glanced over to see her watching him with a sympathetic smile. "Just fine, Lillian. Just fine."

She nodded knowingly. "Looks like the two of you are butting heads a bit. Hopefully, things will get better."

"Let's hope," he said, though he wasn't convinced.

Chapter 6

Stepping out onto the sidewalk, Conner squinted against the afternoon sun. Across the street, the Valley General Store bustled with activity. A couple of teenagers laughed as they skateboarded past, and an elderly couple strolled hand in hand, enjoying the day.

His stomach grumbled, reminding him he'd skipped lunch. Maybe a bite to eat would help clear his head.

He made his way down the street to the Bluebird Café, the local diner that had been a staple in town since before he was born. The bell above the door chimed as he entered, and the aroma of fresh coffee and baked goods enveloped him.

Sliding into a booth by the window, Conner picked up a menu. A perky waitress with light-brown hair approached, a notepad in hand.

"Conner Hart," she said. "Haven't seen you around these parts in a long time. Kind of figured I'd run into you sooner or later."

He looked up, recognition dawning. "Missy Nolan. Been a while."

"It sure has. Didn't think you'd have the guts to show your face back here."

Conner winced inwardly. Rachel's younger sister had never been one to mince words. "Missy, please. It's not been a good day. I'm back. I'm here for good. Let's just leave it at that."

"Fine." She arched an eyebrow. "Well, what can I get you?"

"I'll take a coffee and the cheeseburger platter."

"Coffee and cheeseburger," she repeated, jotting it down. "Coming right up."

As she walked away, Conner couldn't help but feel the weight of scrutiny. The Nolan sisters were tight-knit, and he had no doubt that Rachel would hear about this encounter soon enough.

He stared out the window, watching the world go by. Children with their parents on the sidewalk, shop owners chatted with customers, and the valley's rolling hills loomed in the distance. It all felt so familiar, yet so foreign.

"Here you go." Missy sat down the mug of coffee with a clink. "Food'll be out soon."

"Thanks."

She hesitated for a moment before sliding into the seat across from him. "Hope you don't mind if I sit?"

Conner shrugged. "Suit yourself."

She studied him; her gaze sharp. "So, what's the real reason you're back?"

He met her eyes. "The ranch. That's it. Nothing more."

"Listen, Conner," she began, her tone serious. "Rachel's moved on. She doesn't need you waltzing back into her life and stirring things up."

"I'm not here to cause trouble," he said evenly. "Just trying to do right by the ranch."

"Is that so?"

"Yes."

She eyed him skeptically. "You hurt her once. Don't do it again."

He clenched his jaw, resisting the urge to snap back. "I appreciate your concern, but Rachel can speak for herself."

Missy snorted. "Maybe so. But as her sister, it's my job to look out for her. Don't make me get even angrier at you."

"Noted."

She stood up, tossing her hair over her shoulder. "Just remember what I said."

"I will."

With one last glare, she headed back toward the kitchen.

Conner exhaled slowly, rubbing the back of his neck. This homecoming was proving more complicated than he'd expected. Everywhere he turned, there were reminders of the bridges he'd burned. And now, with Rachel thrust back into his life for the foreseeable future, the past loomed larger than ever.

His burger arrived shortly after, delivered by a different waitress, who offered a polite smile before leaving him to his meal. The first bite was delicious—the flavors of home. As he ate, he allowed his mind to wander.

Memories of afternoons spent riding horses across the open fields flashed through his mind. Rachel's laughter echoing in the wind, her eyes bright with joy. The warmth of the sun on their faces as they dreamed about the future.

He'd been so young then. So foolish.

The ring of his cell phone jolted him back to the present. Fishing it out of his pocket, he glanced at the caller ID.

Judd Franklin.

Great.

He answered reluctantly. "Yeah?"

"Conner," Judd's gruff voice came through the line. "Need you back at the ranch. Got some things to discuss."

"What things?"

"Nothing that can't wait, but sooner's better."

Conner sighed. "Fine. I'll be there in an hour."

"Make it thirty minutes," Judd insisted before hanging up.

Conner stared at the phone, irritation bubbling up. Judd had been less than welcoming since his return, and it seemed the foreman was intent on making his life difficult.

***

Judd was waiting for Conner by the barn, arms crossed over his broad chest. His weathered face was set in a stern expression beneath the brim of his hat.

"You're late," Judd remarked as Conner approached.

"Had to finish my lunch," Conner replied evenly.

Judd grunted. "We need to talk about summer preparations. Many things are overdue. Here we are, at the beginning of June, and many things aren't done. Livestock needs sorting, and there are repairs to be done."

"I thought you had everything under control," Conner said, unable to keep a hint of sarcasm from his tone.

"I do," Judd retorted. "But seeing as you're the boss now, thought you might want to be involved. This is ranch life. There's no time to by messing around in town and wasting time."

Conner studied the older man. There was a challenge in Judd's gaze—a test of sorts. "All right. Let's go over it."

They headed into the barn, the scent of hay and horses enveloping them. The sounds of animals settling in filled the space—a comforting chorus of snorts, whinnies, and rustling.

Judd laid out the plans, detailing the tasks that needed attention. Conner listened attentively, occasionally interjecting with suggestions or questions.

"Your father was a hard man," Judd said. "But he cared about this place. He ran this ranch with an iron fist when he could. His last year or so on earth, he wasn't able to work as much. I've done the best I could. Now it's your turn to step it up and be responsible."

"I know."

"Question is, do you?"

Conner met his gaze steadily. "I'm here, aren't I?"

"Being here and caring and working ain't the same thing."

"I intend to see this through," Conner asserted. "You can count on that."

Judd nodded slowly. "We'll see."

With that, the foreman turned and walked away, leaving Conner alone in the barn.

Exhaling, Conner ran a hand through his hair. It seemed everyone was determined to doubt him. Not that he could blame them. His track record wasn't exactly stellar.

A soft whinny caught his attention. He glanced toward the stalls to see a sleek chestnut mare peering at him over the gate. Her intelligent eyes followed his movements.

"Hey there, girl," he murmured, approaching slowly.

The mare nickered softly, extending her nose toward him. Conner reached out, gently stroking her velvety muzzle.

"Her name's Bella," a voice said from behind him.

He turned to see Rachel standing a few feet away, a bale of hay balanced effortlessly on her shoulder.

"She was skittish when she first arrived," Rachel continued, setting the hay down. "But she's come a long way."

Conner smiled slightly. "She's beautiful."

"She is." Rachel walked over to the stall, offering the horse a carrot from her pocket. "Aren't you, pretty girl?"

An awkward silence settled between them. Conner searched for something to say. "Listen, about earlier—"

"Don't," she interrupted, holding up a hand. "We don't need to get into it."

He frowned. "Rachel, we can't avoid this forever. We're going to be working together."

She sighed, her shoulders sagging slightly. "I know. But that doesn't mean we have to dredge up the past."

"Maybe we should," he insisted. "Clear the air."

She shook her head. "What's the point? It won't change anything."

"Maybe not, but—"

"What's done is done, Conner," she cut him off. "I am sorry for the way I talked to you today in Joel's office. That was out of line and uncalled-for. For that, I'm sorry."

Before he could respond, she turned and walked out of the barn.

Conner leaned against the stall door, frustration gnawing at him. This was going to be harder than he thought.

Bella nudged his arm, her soft eyes seeming to convey sympathy.

"At least someone around here doesn't hate me," he muttered, offering the mare a pat.

Chapter 7

The shed was exactly as Conner remembered it—cluttered but organized in its own way. Tools hung from pegs on the wall, coils of rope were neatly stacked in a corner, and the scent of engine oil and wood shavings filled the air. Conner located a toolbox and gathered the supplies he'd need for the fence repairs: hammer, nails, wire, and a few new planks.

As he loaded the materials into a wheelbarrow, his mind wandered back to his conversation with Judd yesterday morning. The foreman's guarded demeanor was understandable, but it still grated on Conner's nerves. He couldn't blame Judd for being protective of Rachel, especially considering how he'd left things. Still, the man's skepticism only fueled Conner's determination.

He wheeled the barrow toward the south pasture; the path taking him past the paddocks where a few horses watched him with mild interest. The sun climbed higher, warming the chill from the morning air. Birds chirped from the branches overhead, and a pair of butterflies danced lazily around a patch of wildflowers.

Arriving at the fence line, Conner assessed the damage. Several posts were leaning, and the wire was sagging in places, an obvious invitation for curious horses to test their boundaries. He set to work, removing the damaged sections and replacing them with new posts and rails. The physical labor felt good, grounding him in the present and providing a welcome distraction from his tumultuous thoughts.

As he hammered in another nail, he heard footsteps approaching. Turning, he saw Levi Williams strolling up, hands shoved casually into his pockets. Levi tipped his hat in greeting.

"Morning, Conner. Welcome home."

"Levi," Conner replied, wiping sweat from his brow. "How's it going?"

"Not bad. Heard you were out here fixing fences. Thought I'd lend a hand."

Conner offered a grateful smile. "Appreciate it. Could use an extra set of hands."

Levi leaned against a nearby post. "So, you're back for good?"

"That's the plan," Conner said.

"Well, can't say I'm surprised. Took ya long enough, though," Levi rubbed his chin thoughtfully. "Place hasn't been the same without you."

Conner glanced at him in surprise. "Didn't think anyone would notice."

"Hard not to notice when the boss's son goes AWOL," Levi said with a wry grin. "But seriously, folks around here might be skeptical, but I think it's good you're back."

"Thanks," Conner replied, feeling a flicker of hope. "Means a lot coming from you."

Levi shrugged. "Everyone deserves a second chance, buddy. I've surely missed having you around here."

They worked side by side for a while, replacing another section of fencing. Levi filled him in on some of the ranch happenings—the births of new foals, the challenges they'd faced during last winter's storms, and little snippets of life that Conner had missed.

"How's Will doing?" Conner asked.

"Same as ever. Quiet, reliable. He's up in the north pasture checking the water troughs today."

Conner nodded. "Good to hear."

Levi hesitated before speaking again. "Look, Conner, I know things are... going to be complicated around here. Judd will be a bear to deal with."

Conner's hammer paused mid-swing. "That's an understatement. He's already proven he's still got a beef with me."

"Just saying, give it time. And Rachel...she's had a rough go, and your sudden reappearance is bound to stir things up."

"I'm aware, and it already has," Conner said, resuming his work. "I don't expect anything from her. Just hoping to earn back some trust. From you, Will, and Judd as well."

"Fair enough." Levi adjusted his hat. "For what it's worth, I think you coming back is a step in the right direction. I followed your rodeo days, and I'm sorry they ended."

Conner offered a small smile. "Appreciate that."

They finished the repairs by midday, the sun now high overhead. Conner's shirt clung to his back, damp with sweat, but he felt a sense of accomplishment. As they packed up the tools, his stomach growled loudly.

"Hungry?" Levi chuckled.

"Guess I am," Conner admitted. "Been a while since breakfast."

"Why don't you join us at the bunkhouse for lunch? Will should be back by now."

Conner considered the offer. It was another opportunity to reconnect, and he couldn't afford to pass that up. "Sure, sounds good."

They made their way back toward the main cluster of ranch buildings. The bunkhouse was a long, single-story structure with a wide porch and a scattering of worn chairs. The aroma of something delicious wafted from the open doorway.

Inside, Will Shepherd was setting out bowls and plates on a large wooden table. He looked up as they entered, his expression neutral.

"Conner," Will greeted with a nod.

"Will. Good to see you."

Will nodded toward the laden table. "Got enough stew here to feed an army. Grab a bowl."

"Don't mind if I do," Conner said, taking a seat and inhaling the rich aroma. "Sure brings back memories."

"Yep... that it does," Will said, his tone even. "Dig in."

As they filled their bowls, Levi chimed in, "Conner and I tackled that sagging fence down in the south pasture this morning."

"That right?" Will's gaze settled on Conner, a hint of curiosity in his eyes. "Jumping back into ranch work, are you?"

"Figured it's about time I pulled my weight," Conner replied.

Will took a sip of his iced tea. "Place has been running fine without you."

Conner swallowed, sensing the unspoken tension. "I don't doubt that. I'm here to help where I can and pick up where my dad left off."

Will leaned back in his chair. "What's your plan, Conner? Here for a visit, or are you planting roots?"

"Planning to stay," Conner said firmly.

Will considered this, his expression unreadable. "Long road ahead."

"I'm ready for it," Conner said.

Levi clapped a hand on Conner's shoulder. "Told you he'd be back, Will."

Will managed a slight smile. "Guess you were right. Just didn't think it'd take a decade."

Conner looked between them. "Better late than never, I hope."

"We'll see. Actions speak louder than words around here," Will shrugged. "So, what's your plans for the rest of the afternoon?"

Conner paused, the spoon hovering over his bowl, as he considered Will's question. "Figured I'd check on the horses in the east paddock, get familiar with the herd," he said.

Will nodded slowly, his gaze steady. "Got a filly that's been a bit skittish. Rachel's been working with her."

At the mention of Rachel, an uneasy knot formed in Conner's stomach. He hadn't seen her since their tense encounter in the stables. "Maybe I could lend a hand," he offered cautiously. "If she doesn't mind."

Levi's eyes twinkled with a trace of mischief. "Rachel ain't one to refuse help with the horses," he said, stirring his spoon thoughtfully. "But if I were you, I'd watch my step. She's got a way of keeping folks on their toes."

Will shared a brief, knowing glance with Levi before turning back to Conner. "Just be certain you're up for it," he cautioned. "That filly's got a wild streak, and her trainer's no different."

Conner sighed, attempting a casual shrug. "I can handle a spirited horse," he replied. "The trainer... that's a whole other challenge."

A chuckle passed between the men. Will tapped his fingers on the table. "Well, if you're serious about sticking around... best start mending fences as soon as possible, both the wooden kind and the personal."

"I agree," Conner admitted, his gaze dropping to the worn tabletop.

Will softened slightly, a hint of understanding in his eyes. "Helping with that filly is a good place to start. She's a handful, but with patience, she'll come around."

Conner looked up, a flicker of resolve in his eyes as he nodded

He stood to leave, and Levi called after him. "Hey, Conner."

He paused at the doorway. "Yeah?"

"Keep your chin up,"

Conner offered a faint smile. "I'll do my best. And thanks for the meal."

Chapter 8

As Conner approached the paddock, he spotted Rachel near the fence, her blonde hair catching the sunlight as she moved with gentle grace. She was coaxing the young filly to follow her, patience evident in every gesture.

Conner hesitated, suddenly aware of how his presence might unsettle her. But he was here to mend fences—literally and figuratively—and that meant facing everything head-on.

Summoning his resolve, he walked toward her. "Need an extra hand?"

Rachel turned sharply, surprise flashing in her green eyes. "I have work to do, Conner."

"Just wanted to offer my help," he said. "Thought maybe I could lend a hand."

She sighed, keeping her gaze forward. "This is my domain, remember? You go pretend to be a cowboy. I've got this under control."

"I don't doubt that you have everything under control," he replied. "But sometimes an extra perspective can make a difference."

Rachel stopped abruptly and turned to face him. Her eyes bored into his, a mixture of frustration and something else he couldn't quite place. "Why are you doing this?"

"Doing what?"

"Acting like you care," she said, her voice tight. "Offering help, trying to involve yourself."

"Because I do care," Conner said earnestly.

She shook her head. "You can't just waltz back in after all this time and expect everything to be fine."

"I know that," he admitted. "But I have to start somewhere."

Rachel looked at him cautiously. "Suit yourself. This one's a handful."

He approached slowly, keeping a respectful distance. "Did you give her the name Luna?"

"Yes," Rachel replied, her attention returning to the filly. "Found her wandering near the south creek a few months back. No brand, and no one's claimed her."

"She's beautiful," Conner said.

"She doesn't trust easily," Rachel noted, casting a sidelong glance at him. "Can't say I blame her."

Conner swallowed, recognizing the double meaning. "Trust has to be earned."

"That it does."

Rachel led the filly while Conner stood by, offering calm reassurance. Luna's ears flicked back and forth, wary but curious.

"Hold out your hand," Rachel instructed. "Let her come to you."

Conner did as he was told, extending his palm and waiting patiently. Luna sniffed the air, taking a tentative step forward. The warmth of her breath brushed against his skin as she finally made contact.

"There you go," Rachel said, a hint of approval in her tone.

A subtle smile touched Conner's lips. "Guess she's willing to give me a chance."

"Animals are excellent judges of character," she replied, meeting his gaze briefly before looking away.

"Rachel," he began cautiously, "I really am sorry."

She sighed, her shoulders tensing. "Conner, it's not that simple. You can't just walk back into my life and expect everything to go back to the way it was."

"I'm not expecting that," he said earnestly. "I just want the opportunity to prove I've changed."

She studied him for a long moment, the guardedness in her eyes softening just a fraction. "Time will tell."

An awkward silence settled between them, filled only by the soft sounds of Luna munching on hay.

"How's your father been?" Conner asked, searching for neutral ground.

Rachel's expression grew somber. "He passed three years ago."

Conner's face fell. "Rachel, I'm so sorry. I didn't know."

She nodded tightly. "There's a lot you don't know."

The sting of her words cut deep, but he couldn't deny them. "I'd like to change that," he offered.

"Like I said, time will tell." She gave Luna an affectionate pat before stepping away. "I've got work to finish in the stables."

"Mind if I join you?" he asked.

She hesitated, then gave a slight shrug. "Suit yourself. Just don't get in my way."

"I'll do my best," he replied, a flicker of hope sparking within him.

They walked toward the stables, the distance between them both physical and emotional. Conner grappled with a mix of regret and determination. Being near Rachel stirred memories he'd long tried to suppress, the sound of her laughter, the way her eyes lit up when she talked about the horses, the dreams they'd once shared under the endless Montana sky.

Inside the stables, Rachel moved with practiced efficiency, checking on each horse and noting their conditions.

"Hand me that brush," she said, gesturing toward a shelf.

Conner obliged, handing it over. "I remember when we used to race to finish chores," he said lightly.

She paused, a faint smile ghosting across her lips. "You always cheated."

"I did not!" he protested, feigning indignation.

"You'd skip brushing just so you could beat me."

He chuckled. "Alright, maybe once or twice."

She shook her head; the tension easing ever so slightly.

"I miss this," he said. "You, me... just talking and working on the ranch."

She met his gaze, the vulnerability in her eyes taking him by surprise. "Me too.," she said.

Before he could respond, footsteps echoed from the entrance. Judd Franklin stood in the doorway, his eyes narrowing as he took in the scene. "Everything alright here?"

"Just fine," Rachel replied quickly, stepping back. "Conner was helping with Luna."

Judd's gaze hardened as it settled on Conner. "Thought you were fixing fences."

"Finished up this morning," Conner said evenly. "Figured I'd make myself useful elsewhere."

"That so?" Judd's tone carried a challenge. "There's plenty to be done without meddling where you're not needed."

"Judd," Rachel interjected, a warning edge to her voice.

Conner straightened, meeting the foreman's stare. "I'm not here to cause trouble."

Judd snorted. "We'll see about that." He shifted his attention to Rachel. "Got those supply orders ready?"

She nodded. "They're on your desk."

"Good." With a final, disapproving glance at Conner, Judd turned and strode away.

An uncomfortable silence lingered in his wake. Conner let out a slow breath. "He's gotten rougher with age."

"He'll come around," Rachel said, though her tone lacked conviction.

"Will he?" Conner asked. "Will you?"

She looked at him, a myriad of emotions flickering across her face. "I don't know, Conner. You really hurt me when you left."

"I regret that every day," he admitted, his voice thick. "If I could do it all over…"

"But you can't," she said softly. "None of us can."

He nodded, accepting the truth of her words. "All I can do is try to be better now."

She studied him for a moment, then gave a slight nod. "Then keep trying."

Chapter 9

The early evening sun cast long shadows across the Gold Star Ranch's weathered front porch as Conner sat in his father's old rocking chair, the journal resting in his lap. The gold lettering of his father's name catching the fading light. Conner ran his fingers over the worn leather, his coffee growing cold on the porch railing beside him.

Taking a deep breath, he opened the journal to a random page, his father's precise handwriting filling the lines. The entry was dated four years after Conner had left home.

"Watched some old videos today of Conner learning to ride. He couldn't have been more than five, sitting up there on old Thunder like he was born in the saddle. Rachel found the tapes in the office while she was searching for a book on horse remedies. Didn't even know Luella had recorded those moments. Seeing him so small, so determined—it hit me hard. That same determination took him all the way to the rodeo circuit. Guess I was too blind to see it for what it was, a pure gift. Too busy trying to make him into what I wanted, instead of seeing what God had already made him to be."

Conner's throat tightened. He'd never heard his father talk like that—not once in all the years they'd lived under the same roof. The mention of his mother's name, Luella, and the home videos she'd taken stirred something deep in his chest.

He flipped forward a few pages, landing on another entry:

"Conner won big at the Houston Rodeo today. Saw it on TV at Hank's store. Eight seconds on Silver Hurricane—they're calling it the ride of the season. My boy's face was all over the sports channels. Folks in town kept congratulating me, like I had something to do with it. Truth is, I didn't. Been four years since he left, and I'm just now learning to watch his rides without reaching for the bottle afterward. Pastor Sam says pride can be a good thing when it comes from the right place. Maybe he's right. I am proud. Just wish I could tell him."

Conner set the journal down on the porch railing, standing abruptly. He paced the length of the porch, his boots heavy against the wooden planks. The realization that his father had followed his career, had watched his rides, had been proud—it twisted something inside him. All those years, he'd assumed Warren Hart had written him off completely.

Conner closed his eyes, letting out a slow breath. The words on the page didn't match the angry, hard-drinking father he'd left behind. Someone else had written these words, someone who'd followed his career from afar, someone who'd...changed.

The distant rumble of an engine drew his attention. A white pickup truck was making its way up the ranch's drive, kicking up dust in the golden evening light. As it drew closer, Conner recognized Pastor Sam Harlow. Sam was the pastor of the Riverbend Valley Community Church, a building he hadn't stepped foot in since he was a child.

Conner picked up the journal and set it on the small table, trying to ignore the way his heart rate had picked up. The thought of speaking with the pastor was unsettling. Faith, prayer, church—it had always felt like foreign territory, full of words that didn't fit in his hands or his life. But there was no avoiding it now.

Sam parked and stepped out, his tall frame unfolding from the driver's seat, his serene smile unchanged from Conner's memories. His kind eyes and easy smile always put people at ease, whether or not they wanted to be. He wore jeans and a plain button-down shirt, no clerical collar or obvious signs of his profession. Just another Montana man dropping by for a visit.

"Evening, Conner. Welcome home," Sam called out, making his way up the porch steps. "Hope I'm not interrupting."

"Just catching up on some reading." Conner said. "What brings you out this way?"

"I heard you were back in town," Sam said, his voice light with curiosity. "Just thought I'd stop by, catch up a bit, and see how you're settling in." His gaze drifted to the leather-bound book, a glimmer of recognition softening his features. "Warren's journal," he murmured, his tone quieter now. "He wrote in it almost every day these past few years."

Conner leaned against the porch railing, crossing his arms. "Seems like you knew him pretty well."

"I did." Sam settled into one of the wooden chairs, his movements unhurried. "Your father was a regular at Sunday services for the last five or six years. Never missed a week unless he was sick."

The image didn't fit with Conner's memories of Warren Hart—the hard-drinking, harsh-voiced man who'd sneered at anything resembling faith or weakness. "That's... hard to picture."

"I imagine it would be." Sam's voice held no judgment, just quiet understanding. "People can surprise us, Conner. Your daddy became a changed man. It was one of the most beautiful things I've ever witnessed."

"He never went to church when I was growing up," Conner said, the words coming out more defensive than he'd intended. "Not once after Mom died. What changed him?"

Sam leaned forward, resting his elbows on his knees. "Would you believe it started with Rachel?"

Conner's head snapped up.

"She found him passed out in the barn one morning, about a year or so after you left. Instead of just walking away, which plenty would have done, she sat with him until he came around. Then she talked to him, really talked to him, about what he was doing to himself." Sam's eyes grew distant. "Rachel has a way of speaking truth with grace. She invited him to church. She invited him over and over, and he never took her up on it. She never gave up on him. Then Warren began making changes in his life and one Sunday, he and Rachel showed up in church together."

Conner swallowed hard, picturing Rachel being there for his father when he hadn't been. The thought stung more than he cared to admit.

"Warren wasn't a perfect man, Conner. He'd be the first to tell you that. No one is perfect. We're all sinners. Warren hit rock bottom and really looked at his life and the mistakes he'd made. He quit drinking. Started attending AA meetings in the next town over. He was already sober when he joined the church. He was sober the rest of his life."

"Mistakes," Conner echoed, the word bitter on his tongue. "Like me?"

Sam shook his head. "No. He didn't think you were a mistake. Warren actually said several times you were a blessing. He felt his mistake was that he failed you almost your entire life. The chances he missed to be the father you needed. That's what ate at him the most."

Conner turned away, staring out at the darkening pasture, where the shadows stretched long across the grass. His father's regrets were something he wasn't sure if he could deal with, not when his own still sat so heavily on his shoulders.

"You know," Sam continued, his voice gentle, "he kept an entire box of newspaper clippings about your rodeo career. Every competition, every win. He'd bring some of them to prayer group every once in a while, show them off like any proud father would."

A lump formed in Conner's throat. He remembered the journal entry he'd just read about the Houston Rodeo. "Seems like you knew a version of my father I never got to meet."

"It's not too late to know him, Conner." Sam gestured toward the journal. "He left you his words. His heart. Sometimes God works in the spaces between what was and what could have been."

Conner let out a short, humorless laugh. "God? I haven't exactly been on speaking terms with Him lately."

"He's still on speaking terms with you." Sam's smile was warm but knowing. "That's the thing about grace—it doesn't wait for an invitation."

Conner reflected on the journal entries and the thought of his father following his rodeo career. An ache stirred within him, knowing his father had quietly tracked his journey from afar. How could a man who had once been so harsh and hateful transform into someone so entirely different? What had driven his father to change his life?

"Rachel told me about the will," Sam said after a moment. "About the stipulations your father put in place."

"Yeah, well." Conner shifted uncomfortably. "Dad always did like to have the last word."

"Or maybe he was trying to give you both something you need-ed—time and purpose. Your daddy loved Rachel like she was his daughter, Conner. In a way, I guess she filled the void you left when you moved away." Sam stood, stretching slightly. "You know where to find me if you want to talk. I simply came by to make sure you knew that. The doors of Riverbend Valley Community Church are always open, Conner. No pressure, but we've got decent coffee and marginally good company. Your father's favorite seat in the front pew near the window is still empty most Sundays."

Conner rubbed the back of his neck. "I appreciate the offer, Pastor Sam, but I'm not sure if I'm ready for—"

"Sunday morning services?" Sam finished with an understanding nod. "That's alright. I just wanted to make sure you knew you were welcome."

The pastor turned to leave, then paused at the top of the porch steps. "You know, your father really missed you. He loved you very much, Conner."

Conner watched Sam's truck disappear down the drive, dust settling in its wake. The sun had dipped lower, painting the sky in shades of purple, pink, and gold. Behind him, the journal seemed to carry a new intrigue, filled with words he both craved and feared to read.

He picked it up again, running his thumb along the worn edges. The leather was soft from years of handling, marked with the imprints of his father's fingers. How many times had Warren sat in this very spot on this porch, pouring out his thoughts, his regrets, his prayers?

Flipping to a random page, Conner began to read:

"Watched Rachel working with that wild mare today, the one nobody else could get near. She has her mama's gift with horses, sees past their fear of what lies beneath. Reminds me of how she saw past my rough edges all those years ago. God has His own way of sending angels, even to old sinners like me. Been praying for Conner today. Wherever he is, Lord, let him know he's loved. Let him find his way home."

Conner shut the journal abruptly, his vision blurring. The evening air had grown cooler, but that wasn't why he was shivering. Everything he thought he knew about his father, about the past ten years, was shifting like sand beneath his feet.

A horse nickered in the distance, drawing his attention to the training paddock where he knew Rachel would be working tomorrow. Rachel, who had seen good in his father when Conner had given up. Rachel, who had helped Warren find his way to faith while Conner was chasing glory in the rodeo circuit.

Chapter 10

The young filly pranced beside Rachel, eager for whatever the day might bring, as they headed for the paddock. Rachel smiled, patting Luna's sleek neck. The horse had come so far in her training, and with the county show just weeks away—

She rounded the corner of the barn and stopped short. Conner was working on the paddock gate. His shoulders flexed as he adjusted something on the hinge. Tools were scattered at his feet, and the old gate latch lay discarded in the grass.

Rachel's breath caught. Even after two weeks, seeing him here still felt surreal, like a dream she might wake from at any moment. Luna nickered softly, drawing Conner's attention.

He straightened, wiping his hands on his jeans. "Morning, Rachel." His voice carried that careful tone he'd been using lately, like he was afraid of spooking a wild horse. "Luna looks good this morning."

Despite herself, Rachel felt a smile tug at her lips. She gestured toward the gate. "I was planning to work with her in the paddock this morning."

"Perfect timing then." Conner turned back to his work, muscles moving beneath his worn shirt as he tightened the new hinge. "I'm almost finished here. That old latch was hanging by a thread."

Rachel shifted her weight, suddenly aware of how different he looked from the reckless young man who'd left ten years ago. There was a quiet competence in his movements now, a steadiness she hadn't expected to find.

"I didn't realize you'd be out here," she said, immediately regretting how defensive it sounded.

Conner shrugged, focused on his task. "Saw the gate needed fixing." He glanced up, meeting her eyes briefly. "I can finish the rest later?"

"No, it's—" Rachel paused, surprised by the genuine consideration in his voice. "It needed to be done. I just... wasn't expecting it."

Luna tugged at the lead rope, eager to investigate the interesting sounds of metal on metal. Rachel steadied her with a gentle hand, watching as Conner attached the new latch with practiced movements.

"There," Conner said finally, stepping back to test the gates swing. It moved smoothly, without the screech that had plagued it. "Should hold now."

He collected his tools, evidently preparing to leave, and something stirred in Rachel's chest. The careful boundaries she maintained around Conner, the distance she was determined to keep, seemed to falter, if only for a moment.

"Thanks, Conner," she called out as he turned away. "For fixing the gate. It really needed attention."

He paused mid-step, then slowly turned back. There was something in his expression, a determination she hadn't seen before, that made her heart skip. Without a word, he set his tools down and walked back to the paddock. Rachel took an instinctive step backward as he approached. Conner's eyes had a burning, faraway look in them.

"Tell me about my dad," he said abruptly, his voice rough with emotion.

Rachel blinked, caught off guard by the sudden shift. "Well, Conner... what do you want to know?"

Conner ran a hand through his hair, his expression conflicted. "Anything. Just... tell me anything about who he became. The man I didn't know." He leaned against the paddock fence, his knuckles white where they gripped the weathered wood. "Everyone talks about him like he was someone different. Someone better."

Rachel's heart squeezed at the raw honesty in his voice. Luna pressed against her side, sensing her tension, and Rachel absently stroked the filly's neck while gathering her thoughts.

"He was different," she said softly. "The changes didn't happen overnight, but..." She took a deep breath, remembering. "There was this one Sunday morning, about four... maybe five years, after you left. I was getting ready for church when someone knocked on my door."

Conner's eyes never left her face as she spoke. "Dad?"

Rachel nodded. "He was standing there on my porch, looking so uncomfortable in a freshly pressed shirt." She smiled faintly at the memory. "Asked if maybe I wouldn't mind some company that morning."

"Just like that?" Conner's voice was barely above a whisper.

"Well, no." Rachel shifted her weight, remembering the months of quiet conversations that had led to that moment. "I'd been inviting him to church for a while. Ever since..." She hesitated, unsure how much to share.

"Since what?"

"Since the morning, I found him passed out in the barn." The words came out gentler than she'd intended. "He was in a dark place after you left, Conner. We all were, in different ways."

Conner's jaw tightened. "But you stayed. You helped him."

"I couldn't just walk away." Rachel looked down at her boots, scuffed from years of ranch work. "Your father was hurting. Sometimes people need someone to see past their rough edges, you know? To keep showing up, even when they push you away."

Luna nudged her shoulder, and Rachel realized she'd stopped moving. She led the filly in a slow circle, giving herself a moment to collect her emotions.

"That first Sunday," she continued, "we sat in the back pew. Your dad, bless his heart, was stiff as a board. But he came back the next week. And the next. We sort of had this little routine. Your dad just showed up on my doorstep every Sunday morning and came with me. That went on for years until he really started getting sick. Then I would come here every Sunday morning and pick him up for church. Rain or shine, he came with me... until he couldn't." She glanced at Conner, saw the mixture of pain and wonder in his eyes. "It wasn't just about church at first, though. It was about finding his way back to himself. To God. In the end, he did."

"When did he quit drinking?" Conner asked, his voice rough with emotion.

Rachel let Luna graze nearby as she moved closer to the fence where Conner stood. "Before he started coming to church. He'd been going to AA meetings in Bridger Falls for a while by then. Said he couldn't face God's house until he'd faced his demons."

A shadow passed over Conner's features. "I should've been here."

"Maybe. Maybe not. Maybe it took you leaving for him to stop and realize what his life had become. Maybe it took you leaving to find yourself as well." Rachel said softly. "But you're here now, Conner, trying to understand your dad. That would've meant something to him."

The morning breeze stirred the tall grass beyond the paddock, and Rachel watched as Conner absorbed her words. He looked different in that moment—younger somehow, more like the boy she'd once known, before rodeo dreams and broken promises had changed everything.

"He kept every article about your rodeo career," she said. "Had an entire box of clippings in his office. Used to show them to anyone who'd listen."

Conner's head snapped up. "Pastor Sam told me."

"He was proud of you, Conner." The words caught in her throat. "Even if he never figured out how to say it before you left. I'm glad you spoke with Pastor."

"Proud?" Conner laughed, but there was no humor in it. "Of what? His son the failure? The one who crashed and burned?"

"Of his son who had the courage to chase his dreams," Rachel corrected firmly. "Of the talent God gave you."

Luna wandered closer, drawn by the intensity in their voices. Rachel gentled her with a soft touch, aware of how the filly mirrored her own skittish heart—wanting to trust, but ready to bolt at any sudden movement.

"The last time I saw him," Conner said, his voice barely audible, "I told him I never wanted to see him again. That he could keep his ranch and his disappointment." He swallowed hard. "I was so angry."

"He forgave you for that, you know." Rachel's words hung in the morning air between them. "He forgave himself, too, eventually. That's what faith does. It helps us see past our failures to who we could be."

Conner pushed away from the fence, running both hands through his hair as he paced. "I keep finding pieces of him everywhere. In his journal, in stories like yours. Pastor Sam said things about this new person dad had become that just seemed impossible." He stopped, turning to face her. "It's like getting to know a stranger."

"Or maybe," Rachel said carefully, "you're finally getting to know the father you never had growing up. Warren buried himself in the bottle and in grief for so long. The man you knew was the bottle talking. It was anger talking."

Luna whinnied softly, drawing Rachel's attention. The filly's ears were pricked forward, her gentle eyes fixed on Conner. Without thinking, Rachel reached for Luna's lead rope.

"Here," she said, holding it out to him. "She wants to say hello."

Conner hesitated, then stepped forward to take the rope, his fingers brushing against hers. The touch, brief as it was, sent a spark through Rachel's hand. She watched as Luna stretched her neck toward Conner, nostrils flaring as she took in his scent.

"Easy, girl," Conner murmured, and Rachel's heart squeezed at the gentleness in his voice. It was the same tone Warren had used with nervous horses, a gift passed from father to son.

"Your father used to say that God speaks the clearest through His creatures," Rachel said. "That horses especially have a way of healing broken spirits."

Conner stroked Luna's nose, his expression thoughtful. "Sounds like something a different Warren Hart would say."

"The Warren Hart I knew these past ten years? That's exactly who he was." Rachel paused, choosing her next words carefully. "He changed, Conner, because he let God change him. It wasn't easy, and it wasn't quick, but it was real."

The morning sun had risen higher, casting their shadows short against the packed earth of the paddock. In the distance, a meadowlark called, its sweet song carrying across the ranch.

"I don't know if I can be what he became," Conner said finally, handing Luna's lead rope back to Rachel.

"Maybe you're not meant to be." Rachel gathered her courage and met his eyes. "Maybe you're just meant to find your own way back to faith. To who God made you to be."

Something shifted in Conner's expression, a softening around his eyes that made Rachel's heart beat faster. For a moment, she caught a glimpse of the man he could become, the one God might be slowly revealing beneath years of hurt and regret.

"Thanks," he said. "For telling me about dad. For...being there when I wasn't."

Rachel nodded, not trusting her voice. She watched as Conner collected his tools and headed toward the barn, his steps slow.

Luna pressed against her shoulder, offering silent comfort, and Rachel wrapped her arms around the filly's neck.

"Lord," she whispered, closing her eyes, "help me remember that You're in control. That maybe—" her voice caught on the words, "—maybe You had a reason for bringing him home. He's hurting, Lord... please help him."

Chapter 11

C onner's boots thudded against the barn floor as he strode in, thoughts of his dad burning in his mind. The tools he'd been carrying clattered as he dropped them, startling several horses in their stalls. His hands shook as he grabbed his saddle, nearly stumbling under its weight.

Thunder, his father's prized quarter horse, nickered softly as Conner approached his stall. The big bay horse's ears pricked forward, sensing Conner's agitation. Conner worked quickly, his movements jerky and uncertain as he saddled Thunder. His thoughts swirled chaotically with the words from his father's journal that he had read over the past several days.

"Pride can be a good thing when it comes from the right place."

"Been praying for Conner today..."

"Let him find his way home..."

The leather creaked as Conner cinched the saddle tight, perhaps a bit too tight, causing Thunder to dance sideways. "Sorry, boy," he muttered, loosening it slightly. His fingers fumbled with the bridle's buckles, frustration mounting as he struggled with the simple task he'd performed thousands of times before.

He needed to move, to run, to escape the suffocating revelations pressing down on his chest. The man in those journal pages, the man Rachel had just described, that wasn't the father he knew. That wasn't the bitter, hard-drinking Warren Hart who'd sneered at Conner's rodeo dreams and driven him away with harsh words and harder expectations.

Leading Thunder out of the barn, Conner swung into the saddle with practiced ease, despite his inner turmoil. He caught a glimpse of Rachel still in the training paddock with Luna, but he couldn't face her again, couldn't face anyone. With a sharp kick to Thunder's sides, he urged the horse forward, probably faster than he should have.

They thundered past the paddock. He felt her eyes on him but didn't look back, couldn't bear to see the concern he knew would be there. Thunder's hooves pounded against the earth, matching the frantic beating of Conner's heart as they raced across the pasture.

The wind whipped at his face, stinging his eyes that were already burning with unshed tears. His father had watched his rodeo rides. His father had been proud of him. His father had changed—had found faith, had found peace—and Conner had missed it all.

Thunder seemed to know where Conner needed to go, following the trail toward the family cemetery. The old horse slowed as they approached the wrought-iron fence, coming to a stop near the gate.

Conner sat motionless in the saddle for a long moment, staring at the collection of headstones that marked generations of Harts who'd lived and died on this land. Finally, he dismounted, his legs slightly unsteady. He looped Thunder's reins around the fence post, giving the horse's neck a grateful pat.

The gate creaked as he pushed it open; the sound jarring in the sacred quiet. His boots crushed the overgrown grass as he made his way to his mother's headstone.

Luella Marie Hart, beloved wife and mother, gone too soon.

Conner sank to his knees beside the grave, running his fingers over the familiar etching of her name. "Hey, Mama," he whispered, his voice rough. "I really made a mess of things, didn't I?"

The breeze rustled through the aspen and cottonwood leaves overhead, a soft, whispering sound that reminded him of his mother's lullabies. "Dad changed, Mama. He actually changed, and I wasn't here to see it. Rachel was, though. She saw something in him worth saving when I couldn't—or wouldn't."

He glanced at the space beside his mother's grave, the spot where Warren's ashes would soon rest. "I don't even know who he was anymore. The man in his journal, the man that everyone keeps telling me about, that's not the father I remember. He followed my career, Mama. He was proud of me, and I never knew."

Conner's gaze swept over the other headstones—great-grandparents, uncles, cousins, all Harts who'd lived and died believing in this land, in family, in faith. "I'll bring him home to you soon," he promised. "Right here where he belongs. I just..." his voice cracked. "I just wish I'd known. Wish I'd come back before it was too late."

The sound of approaching hoofbeats made him tense, but he didn't turn around. He knew who it would be—who it had to be. Rachel had always known where to find him, even when they were kids.

He heard her dismount, heard the soft creak of the gate hinges. "I kind of thought you were headed this way," she said quietly. "Can I sit with you?"

Conner nodded, not trusting his voice. Rachel settled beside him in the grass, close enough that he could smell the familiar scent of her perfume.

"I still have to go pick up Dad's ashes from the funeral home," he managed after a moment.

Rachel nodded, her eyes on Luella's headstone. "I know."

"Not looking forward to doing that." The words felt inadequate for the mountain of emotion behind them.

"No one ever is," Rachel said softly. Her hand found his in the grass, a gentle pressure that anchored him.

"Guess I need to figure out what day to have a small service for him." Conner swallowed hard. "I don't even know who I should ask to come."

"Ask Judd and the other ranch hands," Rachel suggested. "I'd like to come, if that's okay."

"Of course you can come." Conner turned to look at her, really look at her. The sun caught the gold in her hair, reminding him of countless evenings they'd spent together in this very spot, talking and dreaming of their future. "Rachel..."

"Yes?"

He stumbled over the words. "Will you come with me to pick up Dad? I'm not asking for anything else from you, just... I don't think I can do it alone."

Rachel's hand tightened on his. "Of course I will."

They sat in companionable silence for a while; the breeze stirring the surrounding grass. Conner studied Rachel's profile, wondering at the mystery of her—how she'd seen good in his father when Conner couldn't, how she'd helped Warren find faith when Conner had given up on both of them.

"Why did you stay?" he asked suddenly. "All these years, why didn't you leave Riverbend Valley or even the ranch like I did?"

Rachel turned to meet his gaze, her hazel eyes serious. "Because sometimes staying takes more courage than leaving. There was a reason for my staying. God had a plan, and maybe this is part of it. To help you understand your dad... the real Warren Hart. And... part of me knew you would come back some day."

The words hit him like a physical blow. Before he could respond, Rachel stood, brushing grass from her jeans. "I should get back to Luna. She still needs work on her ground manners."

Conner nodded, watching as she walked back to her horse. She paused at the gate, looking back at him. "When you're ready to go to the funeral home, just let me know."

"Rachel?" He called after her. She turned, waiting. "Thank you. For everything you did for him."

A soft smile touched her lips. "Your father was worth saving, Conner. He just needed someone to believe that."

As Rachel rode away, Conner turned back to his mother's grave. "Mama, dad got so much worse after you left. The drinking. The anger. I think I understand now, Mama," he whispered. "Why you never gave up on him, even when things were at their worst. You saw what he could be, not just what he was."

Conner stood, his legs stiff from kneeling. He traced his mother's name one last time, then looked at the empty space beside her grave.

"I'll bring him home soon, Mama. And maybe..." he glanced in the direction Rachel had ridden, "maybe I've finally found my way home too."

Thunder nickered softly as Conner mounted up, but instead of heading straight back to the barn, he guided Thunder to the trail's edge, looking out over the ranch that stretched before him.

This land had shaped generations of Harts, had witnessed their triumphs and failures, their beginnings and endings. His father had found redemption here, had found faith in something bigger than himself.

The ride back to the barn was slower, more thoughtful than his wild dash out. As they approached the barn, Conner saw Rachel in the paddock, working patiently with Luna.

Conner dismounted and led Thunder into the barn, taking his time brushing her with care. As he worked, he remembered other times like this one—helping his father groom the horses, learning the proper way to check hooves and apply liniment to tired muscles. Had there been love there, underneath all the criticism and expectations?

Rachel's voice drifted in from outside, speaking softly to Luna as she led the filly to her stall. Conner paused in his work, listening to the gentle tone that had somehow reached through his father's defenses when nothing else could.

"She's coming along nicely," he said as Rachel passed Thunder's stall.

She stopped, offering him a small smile. "She just needs patience and consistency. Most broken things do."

The words hung between them, heavy with meaning. Conner cleared his throat. "Look, about earlier..."

"You don't have to explain," Rachel interrupted gently. "Grief doesn't follow any rules, Conner. It comes in waves, and sometimes you just have to ride them out."

He nodded, grateful for her understanding. "Still, thank you for following me out there. And for agreeing to come with me to the funeral home."

"That's what friends do." She hesitated, then added, "We were friends once, before everything else. Maybe we can be again."

Friends. The word felt both like a step forward and a step back, but Conner knew he had no right to expect more. Not yet. Maybe not ever. "I'd like that," he said honestly.

Rachel's smile widened slightly. "Good. Now, how about you help me get Luna settled? She seems to respond well to your voice."

They worked together in comfortable silence, moving around each other with ease. It reminded Conner of countless evenings spent just like this, before dreams of rodeo glory and horrible words and quick judgements had tempted him away. Before, he'd chosen the roar of the crowd over the quiet contentment of home.

As they finished up, Rachel paused in the barn doorway. "I'll talk to Pastor Sam tomorrow about the service if you'd like. I know he'd be honored to say a few words."

Conner tensed slightly at the mention of the pastor, but nodded. "Dad would have wanted that, I guess. Since he was going to church and all."

"Your father found a lot of peace in his faith," Rachel said carefully. "It helped him face his demons, accept forgiveness. Both God's forgiveness and his own."

"Seems like everyone knew a version of my father I never got to meet," Conner said, the words coming out more bitter than he'd intended.

Rachel touched his arm lightly. "Maybe getting to know that version of him now, even after he's gone, is part of God's plan. Sometimes the lessons we need most come in unexpected ways."

"Will you come with me now..." Conner asked. "I mean... to go pick up Dad?"

"Of course I will," she replied without hesitation.

Chapter 12

Conner's boots thudded against the barn floor as he strode in, thoughts of his dad burning in his mind. The tools he'd been carrying clattered as he dropped them, startling several horses in their stalls. His hands shook as he grabbed his saddle, nearly stumbling under its weight.

Thunder, his father's prized quarter horse, nickered softly as Conner approached his stall. The big bay horse's ears pricked forward, sensing Conner's agitation. Conner worked quickly, his movements jerky and uncertain as he saddled Thunder. His thoughts swirled chaotically with the words from his father's journal that he had read over the past several days.

"Pride can be a good thing when it comes from the right place."

"Been praying for Conner today..."

"Let him find his way home..."

The leather creaked as Conner cinched the saddle tight, perhaps a bit too tight, causing Thunder to dance sideways. "Sorry, boy," he muttered, loosening it slightly. His fingers fumbled with the bridle's buckles, frustration mounting as he struggled with the simple task he'd performed thousands of times before.

He needed to move, to run, to escape the suffocating revelations pressing down on his chest. The man in those journal pages, the man Rachel had just described, that wasn't the father he knew. That wasn't the bitter, hard-drinking Warren Hart who'd sneered at Conner's rodeo dreams and driven him away with harsh words and harder expectations.

Leading Thunder out of the barn, Conner swung into the saddle with practiced ease, despite his inner turmoil. He caught a glimpse of Rachel still in the training paddock with Luna, but he couldn't face her again, couldn't face anyone. With a sharp kick to Thunder's sides, he urged the horse forward, probably faster than he should have.

They thundered past the paddock. He felt her eyes on him but didn't look back, couldn't bear to see the concern he knew would be there. Thunder's hooves pounded against the earth, matching the frantic beating of Conner's heart as they raced across the pasture.

The wind whipped at his face, stinging his eyes that were already burning with unshed tears. His father had watched his rodeo rides. His father had been proud of him. His father had changed—had found faith, had found peace—and Conner had missed it all.

Thunder seemed to know where Conner needed to go, following the trail toward the family cemetery. The old horse slowed as they approached the wrought-iron fence, coming to a stop near the gate.

Conner sat motionless in the saddle for a long moment, staring at the collection of headstones that marked generations of Harts who'd lived and died on this land. Finally, he dismounted, his legs slightly unsteady. He looped Thunder's reins around the fence post, giving the horse's neck a grateful pat.

The gate creaked as he pushed it open; the sound jarring in the sacred quiet. His boots crushed the overgrown grass as he made his way to his mother's headstone.

Luella Marie Hart, beloved wife and mother, gone too soon.

Conner sank to his knees beside the grave, running his fingers over the familiar etching of her name. "Hey, Mama," he whispered, his voice rough. "I really made a mess of things, didn't I?"

The breeze rustled through the aspen and cottonwood leaves overhead, a soft, whispering sound that reminded him of his mother's lullabies. "Dad changed, Mama. He actually changed, and I wasn't here to see it. Rachel was, though. She saw something in him worth saving when I couldn't—or wouldn't."

He glanced at the space beside his mother's grave, the spot where Warren's ashes would soon rest. "I don't even know who he was anymore. The man in his journal, the man that everyone keeps telling me about, that's not the father I remember. He followed my career, Mama. He was proud of me, and I never knew."

Conner's gaze swept over the other headstones—great-grandparents, uncles, cousins, all Harts who'd lived and died believing in this land, in family, in faith. "I'll bring him home to you soon," he promised. "Right here where he belongs. I just..." his voice cracked. "I just wish I'd known. Wish I'd come back before it was too late."

The sound of approaching hoofbeats made him tense, but he didn't turn around. He knew who it would be—who it had to be. Rachel had always known where to find him, even when they were kids.

He heard her dismount, heard the soft creak of the gate hinges. "I kind of thought you were headed this way," she said quietly. "Can I sit with you?"

Conner nodded, not trusting his voice. Rachel settled beside him in the grass, close enough that he could smell the familiar scent of her perfume.

"I still have to go pick up Dad's ashes from the funeral home," he managed after a moment.

Rachel nodded, her eyes on Luella's headstone. "I know."

"Not looking forward to doing that." The words felt inadequate for the mountain of emotion behind them.

"No one ever is," Rachel said softly. Her hand found his in the grass, a gentle pressure that anchored him.

"Guess I need to figure out what day to have a small service for him." Conner swallowed hard. "I don't even know who I should ask to come."

"Ask Judd and the other ranch hands," Rachel suggested. "I'd like to come, if that's okay."

"Of course you can come." Conner turned to look at her, really look at her. The sun caught the gold in her hair, reminding him of countless evenings they'd spent together in this very spot, talking and dreaming of their future. "Rachel..."

"Yes?"

He stumbled over the words. "Will you come with me to pick up Dad? I'm not asking for anything else from you, just... I don't think I can do it alone."

Rachel's hand tightened on his. "Of course I will."

They sat in companionable silence for a while; the breeze stirring the surrounding grass. Conner studied Rachel's profile, wondering at the mystery of her—how she'd seen good in his father when Conner couldn't, how she'd helped Warren find faith when Conner had given up on both of them.

"Why did you stay?" he asked suddenly. "All these years, why didn't you leave Riverbend Valley or even the ranch like I did?"

Rachel turned to meet his gaze, her hazel eyes serious. "Because sometimes staying takes more courage than leaving. There was a reason for my staying. God had a plan, and maybe this is part of it. To help you understand your dad... the real Warren Hart. And... part of me knew you would come back some day."

The words hit him like a physical blow. Before he could respond, Rachel stood, brushing grass from her jeans. "I should get back to Luna. She still needs work on her ground manners."

Conner nodded, watching as she walked back to her horse. She paused at the gate, looking back at him. "When you're ready to go to the funeral home, just let me know."

"Rachel?" He called after her. She turned, waiting. "Thank you. For everything you did for him."

A soft smile touched her lips. "Your father was worth saving, Conner. He just needed someone to believe that."

As Rachel rode away, Conner turned back to his mother's grave. "Mama, dad got so much worse after you left. The drinking. The anger. I think I understand now, Mama," he whispered. "Why you never gave up on him, even when things were at their worst. You saw what he could be, not just what he was."

Conner stood, his legs stiff from kneeling. He traced his mother's name one last time, then looked at the empty space beside her grave.

"I'll bring him home soon, Mama. And maybe..." he glanced in the direction Rachel had ridden, "maybe I've finally found my way home too."

Thunder nickered softly as Conner mounted up, but instead of heading straight back to the barn, he guided Thunder to the trail's edge, looking out over the ranch that stretched before him.

This land had shaped generations of Harts, had witnessed their triumphs and failures, their beginnings and endings. His father had found redemption here, had found faith in something bigger than himself.

The ride back to the barn was slower, more thoughtful than his wild dash out. As they approached the barn, Conner saw Rachel in the paddock, working patiently with Luna.

Conner dismounted and led Thunder into the barn, taking his time brushing her with care. As he worked, he remembered other times like this one—helping his father groom the horses, learning the proper way to check hooves and apply liniment to tired muscles. Had there been love there, underneath all the criticism and expectations?

Rachel's voice drifted in from outside, speaking softly to Luna as she led the filly to her stall. Conner paused in his work, listening to the gentle tone that had somehow reached through his father's defenses when nothing else could.

"She's coming along nicely," he said as Rachel passed Thunder's stall.

She stopped, offering him a small smile. "She just needs patience and consistency. Most broken things do."

The words hung between them, heavy with meaning. Conner cleared his throat. "Look, about earlier..."

"You don't have to explain," Rachel interrupted gently. "Grief doesn't follow any rules, Conner. It comes in waves, and sometimes you just have to ride them out."

He nodded, grateful for her understanding. "Still, thank you for following me out there. And for agreeing to come with me to the funeral home."

"That's what friends do." She hesitated, then added, "We were friends once, before everything else. Maybe we can be again."

Friends. The word felt both like a step forward and a step back, but Conner knew he had no right to expect more. Not yet. Maybe not ever. "I'd like that," he said honestly.

Rachel's smile widened slightly. "Good. Now, how about you help me get Luna settled? She seems to respond well to your voice."

They worked together in comfortable silence, moving around each other with ease. It reminded Conner of countless evenings spent just like this, before dreams of rodeo glory and horrible words and quick judgements had tempted him away. Before, he'd chosen the roar of the crowd over the quiet contentment of home.

As they finished up, Rachel paused in the barn doorway. "I'll talk to Pastor Sam tomorrow about the service if you'd like. I know he'd be honored to say a few words."

Conner tensed slightly at the mention of the pastor, but nodded. "Dad would have wanted that, I guess. Since he was going to church and all."

"Your father found a lot of peace in his faith," Rachel said carefully. "It helped him face his demons, accept forgiveness. Both God's forgiveness and his own."

"Seems like everyone knew a version of my father I never got to meet," Conner said, the words coming out more bitter than he'd intended.

Rachel touched his arm lightly. "Maybe getting to know that version of him now, even after he's gone, is part of God's plan. Sometimes the lessons we need most come in unexpected ways."

"Will you come with me now..." Conner asked. "I mean... to go pick up Dad?"

"Of course I will," she replied without hesitation.

Chapter 13

The lunch crowd was in full swing at the Bluebird Café, and conversations dipped momentarily as heads turned toward the door. Conner felt the weight of their stares, some curious, others openly suspicious.

Missy Nolan spotted them immediately from behind the counter, her sharp blue eyes narrowing as she took in the unlikely trio. She set down the coffeepot she'd been holding with deliberate slowness, brushing her hands on her blue apron before making her way over.

"Well, if it isn't my favorite sister," Missy said warmly, giving Rachel a quick side hug before nodding at Judd. "And our favorite grumpy foreman." Her smile cooled several degrees as her gaze landed on Conner. "Didn't expect to see you darkening our door anytime soon again."

"Missy," Rachel warned softly, but her sister ignored her.

"Booth or table?" Missy asked, already gathering menus, though her eyes remained fixed on Conner with an intensity that reminded him of a hawk watching its prey.

"Booth," Judd answered, his gruff voice cutting through the tension. "Corner one, if you've got it."

They followed Missy to a booth tucked in the back corner. Rachel slid in first, and Conner hesitated for a split second before joining her. Judd settled in across from them, his weathered hands immediately reaching for the menu, though Conner suspected the old foreman had it memorized.

"Coffee all around?" Missy asked, her pen poised over her order pad.

"Please," Rachel nodded, then added with a small smile, "And Judd takes his with cream now. He's not as tough as he pretends to be."

"That was our secret," Judd muttered, earning a genuine laugh from Rachel.

"Oh, honey," Missy's voice dripped with false sweetness, staring directly at Conner as she continued. "I don't think anyone's got any secrets left in this town, not even our returning bad boy." She turned on her heel, leaving Conner to absorb the sting of her words.

"Don't mind her," Rachel said quietly. "She's... overly protective."

"More like a rattler waiting to strike," Judd commented, not looking up from his menu. "But she makes the best darn cobblers in three counties, so we tolerate her."

The comment drew a smile from both Rachel and Conner, easing some of the tension. Conner opened his menu, though the offerings blurred before his eyes. He was acutely aware of Rachel beside him. Their elbows brushed as she reached for her water glass.

Missy returned with their coffee, setting Conner's down last with perhaps more force than necessary. A bit sloshed over the rim, but Conner didn't comment, just reached for the cream and sugar she'd brought.

"Ready to order?" she asked, her pen hovering expectantly. "Or do you need more time to decide what you want?" The last part was directed at Conner with unmistakable emphasis.

"I'll have my usual," Rachel said quickly, trying to deflect her sister's attention.

"Chicken fried steak," Judd announced, folding his menu. "Extra gravy."

"And you?" Missy turned to Conner, one eyebrow raised. "Still remember how to order, or has rodeo life made you forget your manners along with everything else?"

Conner kept his voice level, determined not to rise to the bait. "Burger, please. Medium well."

"How domestic," Missy remarked. "There was a time you wouldn't settle for anything less than the most expensive steak on the menu." She gathered their menus with quick, efficient movements. "Course, that was back when you were somebody."

"Missy!" Rachel's voice cracked like a whip. "That's enough."

"Just making conversation," Missy said innocently, but her eyes glittered with challenge. "I'd love to hear all about your rodeo days, Conner. All those buckles and prizes. Guess those don't mean much now, do they?"

Conner took a slow sip of his coffee, buying time to steady his voice. "No, they don't Missy."

"Hmph." Missy said as she started to turn away, then paused. "You know, it's funny. Warren used to sit right where you are now, reading about your rides in the rodeo magazines. Telling everyone who would listen about how proud he was of you. Even when you couldn't be bothered to come home. You should be ashamed of yourself, Conner Hart."

The words hit Conner like a physical blow. He stared down at his coffee cup, his throat tight. Rachel's hand found his knee under the table, a brief, comforting pressure that disappeared as quickly as it came.

"That's quite enough," Rachel said firmly. "We're here for lunch, Missy, not a trip down memory lane."

"Just thought he should know," Missy shrugged, but something in Rachel's tone must have gotten through because she headed off toward the kitchen without another word.

Silence settled over their booth. Conner could feel Rachel's eyes on him and Judd's measuring gaze. He forced himself to look up, to face them both.

"She's not wrong," he said.

"No," Judd agreed, surprising them both with his gentleness. "But she ain't entirely right either. Man's got a right to make things good in his life again. We all make mistakes and don't need 'em shoved down our throats every minute of the day."

Rachel nodded, her shoulder brushing against Conner's as she reached for her coffee. "And some people," she added with a pointed look toward the kitchen, "need to remember that grace goes both ways."

The conversation shifted then, with Judd bringing up some necessary repairs to the north pasture fence. Conner listened gratefully as Rachel and Judd discussed ranch business. Every now and then, he'd catch Rachel sneaking glances at him, her expression thoughtful.

Their food arrived with minimal commentary from Missy, though she couldn't resist one last parting shot. "Careful with that burger," she told Conner. "Wouldn't want you choking on your pride."

"For heaven's sake," Rachel muttered, setting down her fork with a clatter. "Missy, can I talk to you for a minute? In private?"

Before her sister could object, Rachel was sliding out of the booth, forcing Conner to move to let her pass. He caught a whiff of her perfume again as she brushed by him, then watched as she practically marched Missy toward the kitchen like a child needing disciplined.

"Well," Judd said, cutting into his chicken fried steak, "that ought to be interesting."

Through the kitchen's swinging door, Conner could see the sisters engaged in what appeared to be an intense discussion. Rachel's shoulders were set in a stubborn line that he remembered all too well.

"Your food's getting cold," Judd observed, drawing Conner's attention back to the booth. "And watching those two won't make it any warmer."

Conner picked up his burger, but his appetite had disappeared. "How do you do it, Judd?"

"Do what?"

"Stay so... neutral in all this."

Judd chewed thoughtfully for a moment before answering. "Ain't about being neutral, boy. It's about watching and waiting. Your daddy taught me that."

"Really?" Conner couldn't keep the skepticism from his voice.

"Yeah, really." Judd set down his fork and fixed Conner with a steady gaze. "The man you knew as your father and the man I knew these last few years... they weren't the same person. Warren learned to watch and wait. To trust in God's timing." He picked up his fork again. "Course, took him hitting rock bottom first."

Before Conner could respond, Rachel returned to the booth, her cheeks flushed. Missy was nowhere in sight.

"Everything okay?" Conner asked, as he let her slide back in.

"Fine," Rachel said shortly, then softened. "She just... she needs to remember that not everyone's story is finished being written yet. We all make mistakes. Not a one of us is perfect."

Conner studied Rachel's profile as she returned to her meal, wondering how she could still have such faith in people, in him, after everything that he had done. How could she so easily forgive and move on?

"Speaking of stories," Judd said, clearing his throat, "remember that time Rachel here had to rescue that fool colt from the creek?"

Rachel groaned, but smiled. "Which time?"

"The time you ended up just as wet as the horse," Judd chuckled. "What was that colt's name? The one attitude problem?"

"Thundercloud," Rachel supplied, her eyes twinkling. "And he didn't have an attitude problem. He was just... spirited."

"Spirited?" Judd snorted. "That horse was possessed. But you wouldn't give up on him."

"She never does," Conner said quietly, the words slipping out before he could stop them.

Rachel turned to look at him. Something soft and undefined passing between them. The moment stretched, broken only when Missy appeared at their table with fresh coffee.

"Dessert?" she asked, her tone notably more subdued. Her eyes flickered to Rachel briefly before settling on Conner. "The apple pie's fresh out of the oven."

"Dad's favorite," Conner said, remembering his father's sweet tooth.

Something flickered across Missy's face. Surprise, perhaps, or the faintest hint of approval. "Yes," she said, her voice losing some of its edge. "He'd come in every Thursday for a slice."

"Three slices of apple pie," Rachel decided, speaking for the group.

Missy's lips twitched into a smile. "I'll grab some ice cream to go with it. On the house."

As she walked away, Conner glanced at Rachel. "Thursday pie runs?"

"Your father had quite a few routines," she explained. "Church on Sundays, pie on Thursdays, Bible study on Wednesday nights."

"And checking the rodeo standings first thing every Monday morning," Judd added. "Never missed it."

The pie arrived steaming, vanilla ice cream already melting at its edges. Conner took a bite and was instantly transported back to the Sunday dinners of his childhood before everything went wrong. His mother had made pie just like this.

"Good?" Rachel asked, watching him.

"Yeah," he managed. "Really good."

They finished their pie in companionable silence. The earlier tension dissolved into something more contemplative. Missy brought the check and set it down without commentary. Conner picked it up and noticed she hadn't charged them for the pie.

As they prepared to leave, Conner heard a snippet of whispered conversation from a nearby table: "...just like his daddy, mark my words. That ranch'll be in ruins within the year..."

Rachel's hand touched his arm lightly. "Hey," she said softly. "Don't listen to them. They don't know the real you."

"Do you?" The question slipped out before he could stop it.

Rachel's eyes met his, steady and clear. "I'm starting to think maybe I never stopped knowing the real you, Conner Hart. I just needed a reminder."

Judd cleared his throat pointedly, reminding them they weren't alone.

At the register, Conner insisted on paying despite Judd's protests. As he waited for his change, Missy leaned across the counter.

"Listen up, rodeo star," she said, quiet enough that only he could hear. "My sister sees something in you worth saving. Don't prove her wrong this time."

It wasn't forgiveness, but it was something close to a chance. Conner nodded solemnly. "I won't, Missy."

Chapter 14

Judd's truck kicked up dust as they pulled into the ranch yard. Conner sat quietly in the middle seat, Warren's urn cradled carefully between his legs on the seat.

Judd killed the engine, and Conner cleared his throat. "Hold up a minute," he said, his voice rougher than he'd intended. "Could you both... would you mind coming with me to the office? There's something I need to do."

Rachel turned to look at him, concern flickering across her features. "Of course."

Judd nodded, leaving the key in the ignition but settling back in his seat. "Whatever you need, boy."

Conner pulled out his phone, thumbs hovering over the screen for a moment, before typing out a brief message to Levi and Will. "Need you both in Minnie's office. Important." He waited until he saw the message marked as delivered before pocketing the phone.

"Levi and Will are coming too," he said, more to himself than the others.

Minnie glanced up as they entered the ranch office, her welcoming smile faltering slightly as she took in their solemn expressions. "Everything alright?" she asked, pushing her glasses up.

Conner stepped forward, the velvet bag containing the urn held carefully in both hands. "I, uh..." He paused, gathering his courage. "I brought Dad home."

Understanding dawned in Minnie's eyes as he gently set the urn on her desk. Her hand flew to her mouth, tears welling up immediately.

"Oh," she whispered, reaching out to touch the velvet bag with trembling fingers. "Oh, Warren..."

The door opened again as Levi and Will arrived, their boots scuffing to a halt as they read the room's atmosphere.

"I miss him so much," Minnie said, her voice breaking. She dabbed at her eyes with a tissue from her desk. "He wasn't perfect, Lord knows, but he was such a good man, especially these last few years. Always telling us about God's grace and second chances, even when we questioned things ourselves."

Conner's throat tightened.

"That's why I asked you all here," Conner managed. "I want... I need to do this right. Dad deserves a proper goodbye, and I'd like your help to plan it."

"Of course," Will said immediately.

"When were you thinking about having it?" Judd asked, his gruff voice gentler than usual.

Conner looked around at the faces gathered in Minnie's office—people who'd known his father better in these last years than he had. "I was thinking Sunday," he said. "After you all get done at church. Something small, just us."

"Sunday afternoon would be perfect," Rachel said softly.

"We could do a small service by the old cottonwood grove next to the cemetery," Levi suggested. "Your dad always liked it out there. Said it reminded him of your mom, Conner."

Conner nodded, surprised by the sudden heat he felt flush on his face. "Yeah, he... he used to take me fishing in the river there when I was little. We'd sit and have lunch on the bench near the cemetery. Then before we left to get back to work on the ranch, dad would go talk to mom. As a kid, I always wondered why he talked to a headstone. Now, I get it."

"It's a good spot," Judd said. "Private, peaceful."

"We'll need to prepare the site in the cemetery," Will pointed out practically. "Ground's hard this time of year."

"I'll handle that," Conner started, but Judd cut him off.

"We'll handle it," the foreman corrected. "Together. That's how we do things around here."

"It's Friday," Levi added. "We've got time now, if you want to get started."

Conner looked at the men, something tight in his chest loosening at their ready acceptance, their willingness to help. His gaze shifted to the urn on Minnie's desk.

"Minnie," he said hesitantly, "would it... would it be okay if Dad stayed here with you until Sunday? In the office?"

Minnie's eyes welled up again, but she smiled through her tears. "I'd be honored, Conner. We spent a lot of time in this office together, your father and me. Planning, dreaming about the ranch's future." She touched the velvet bag again. "He never gave up hope that you'd come home one day."

The words hit Conner like a physical blow.

"We should get started on the site," Judd said, reading the moment. "Daylight's burning, and that ground won't dig itself."

"I'll grab shovels from the equipment shed," Will offered.

"And I've got a thermos of coffee," Levi added with a small grin. "Might need it."

Conner nodded, grateful for their practical approach. He turned to Rachel. "Will you...?"

"Help," she said.

"If you don't mind, I'd rather do this with the guys, but I don't want to exclude you if you'd rather help. I understand if you want to come with us."

"It's okay, I get it. I'll stay here with Minnie for a little while."

"Alright then," Judd said, already heading for the door. "Let's get to it while we've got daylight."

Will and Levi followed Judd out the door. Conner lingered for a moment, looking at the urn that held all that remained of his dad.

"He's home now," Minnie said gently. "Where he belongs. Just like you."

Conner's throat worked. "Thank you, Minnie. For everything."

"Go on." She shooed him with a watery smile. "Those boys'll need your help, even if they won't admit it."

As Conner turned to leave, he caught Rachel watching him, her expression soft and contemplative. Their eyes held for a moment, years of history and hurt and hope passing between them.

"I'll see you later?" he asked.

Rachel nodded. "I'll be here."

Conner stepped out into the late afternoon sun. He could see Judd, Will, and Levi heading toward the equipment shed.

***

Through the office window, Rachel watched the men's figures grow smaller as they headed toward the cemetery on horse back, shovels slung over their shoulders. The late afternoon light painted everything in tones of gold, making even the ordinary scene seem somehow sacred.

"He's changed," Minnie said quietly from her desk. "He's not the same footloose and fancy-free boy that left here."

Rachel turned from the window, finding the older woman arranging papers around Warren's urn, as if making space for an honored guest. "Has he?"

"Oh, honey." Minnie's knowing look carried years of wisdom. "You wouldn't be looking at him like that if he hadn't."

Heat crept into Rachel's cheeks. She settled into the worn leather chair across from Minnie's desk, the same chair where she'd sat countless times before, discussing ranch business and life with Warren.

"Sometimes I look at him and see the boy who broke my heart. Other times..."

"Other times you see the man he is now," Minnie finished. She absent-mindedly straightened a stack of invoices. "Warren saw it too, you know. Even when Conner was gone."

"What do you mean?"

"Warren's last few years... he'd come into my office first thing in the morning when I got here. Often he'd mention something about Conner or tell me a little story. We'd read the bible together. We prayed together for Conner every morning. Warren never stopped believing in his son. Said God wasn't finished with his boy yet. Warren was so proud of him," Minnie said, glancing at the urn.

Rachel's throat tightened. "I didn't know that."

"Course you didn't. Warren kept those little private times between me, him and the Lord." Minnie's eyes grew distant. "But he knew his son would come home someday. And God knew he'd need good people around him when he did."

Chapter 15

Conner drove his shovel into the earth with measured force. The ground was hard, resistant, but not impossible. Kind of like forgiveness, he thought wryly.

"Your old man would've appreciated this," Judd said, working beside him. "Us doing the work ourselves instead of hiring it out."

"Seems right," Will agreed. "Personal."

Levi paused in his digging, leaning on his shovel. "Remember when he used to say manual labor was good for the soul?"

"Usually, right before he put us to work fixing something," Will chuckled.

"Man loved his metaphors," Judd added. "Everything was a lesson with Warren."

Conner listened to their stories, their uninhibited laughter, feeling like an outsider looking in on memories he should have been part of. He drove his shovel deeper, muscles burning.

"You're gonna wear yourself out if you keep hitting it that hard," Judd warned. "Pace yourself, boy. We've got time."

Conner ignored him and kept going. The three men sensed Conner needed to work and work hard, so they silently helped.

The sun had moved noticeably lower in the sky as the men continued their work. The hole was taking shape, each shovelful of earth bringing them closer to completion. Sweat darkened their shirts.

"Your daddy started finding his way back to God right here, beside your mama," Judd said suddenly, wiping his brow.

Conner stopped digging, looking up. "What?"

"He did. I know in my heart it was right here," Judd said, his voice steady. "I found him out here one day, stone-cold sober, talking to God like they were lifelong friends." He motioned to the cottonwoods enveloping the clearing. "Said something about the way the light filtered through the leaves—it reminded him of God's goodness and grace."

Will nodded thoughtfully. "Rachel had been talking to him about faith and God for a while by that point. She'd been inviting him to church for months and never gave up on him."

Conner's hands tightened on the shovel handle.

"That girl," Judd said carefully, "she never gave up on either of you Hart men, Conner. Even when most people would have."

Conner looked up at Judd and said, "So you're telling me she never gave up on me?"

"No, I don't think she ever did. In the first few years after you were gone, she clung tightly to hope, waiting for you to return. As time passed, I think that hope in her heart started to fade a little. But now and then, I'd catch her lost in memories, and she'd mention you. I don't think she ever truly gave up on you," Judd said.

Conner pondered that for a moment. What kind of woman held on to hope after the man she'd loved and had been with for over two years suddenly walked away? Most people would have crumbled, let bitterness wrap around their heart like a fortress. But not Rachel. No, her soul still radiated light, even through the cracks. He wondered if she had cried herself empty enough times that she finally handed the pieces to God to put back together. The thought made his throat tighten.

The sun was touching the mountains when they finally finished. Conner stood at the edge of the grave, looking down at their work. It was deep enough, wide enough, everything measured and prepared with care.

Judd put a hand on Conner's shoulder. "You did good work today, son. Your daddy would be proud."

Conner nodded, not trusting his voice. The four men stood in silence for a moment, the cottonwood and aspen leaves whispering overhead, the cooling air carrying the scent of sage and earth.

"Reckon we should head back," Judd said finally. "Light's failing."

They gathered their tools, bodies tired, but spirits lifted by the shared labor. As they rode back toward the ranch buildings, Conner glanced over his shoulder at the cemetery. The setting sun painted the leaves gold, like grace made visible.

***

Conner's muscles ached from the work, but it was a good ache—the kind that came from doing something meaningful.

Through the office window, warm light spilled out into the gathering dusk. He could see Rachel and Minnie still inside, their heads bent together in conversation. Something about the scene made his heart twist. These women had known his father in ways he hadn't, had been there and stood by him when he hadn't.

"You need anything else?" Judd asked, breaking into his thoughts.

Conner shook his head. "No, I think we're good. Thanks, all of you."

"That's what family does," Will said.

"Family," Conner repeated, testing the word. It felt foreign on his tongue, but not unwelcome.

Levi clapped him on the shoulder. "Get some rest, Hart. Tomorrow's another day."

Conner watched as Judd walked to his truck, and Will and Levi headed to the bunkhouse.

Conner turned at the sound of the office door creaking, watching as Rachel descended the porch steps. She paused when she saw him, and for a moment, they just looked at each other.

"I imagine that was tough on you to do," she said finally.

"Yeah." He said. "We got it done, though."

"You okay?" She took a step closer.

The question was simple, but it reached into places in his heart he'd been trying to ignore. "I don't know," he admitted. "Everything feels... different."

"Different how?"

Conner searched for the words. "Like... like I'm seeing everything in a new way... a different light, maybe. The ranch, Dad, you..." He trailed off, uncertain.

Rachel's expression softened. "Maybe that's not a bad thing."

"No," he agreed quietly. "Maybe not."

Somewhere in the distance, a coyote called, its lonely song echoing across the valley.

"I should go," Rachel said. "It's getting late."

"Rachel?" Conner called, as she turned away. She looked back, waiting. "Thanks again. For going with me today. For... everything."

She nodded, a small smile touching her lips. "Get some rest, Conner. I'll see you tomorrow."

He watched her walk to her truck and continued to watch until her taillights disappeared down the ranch road. The stars were coming out, pinpricks of light in the deepening blue of the Montana sky.

Chapter 16

Felicia sat hunched over the dining room table, a rainbow of colored pens scattered around her alongside a stack of student papers. Her auburn hair was pulled into a loose ponytail, a few stray strands framing her face as she meticulously reviewed each page.

Rachel leaned against the doorway, crossing her arms with a playful smirk. "Hard at work this evening? Those seven-year-olds giving you a run for your money?"

Felicia looked up, a mock exasperated expression on her face. "You joke, but these spelling tests are no laughing matter. You'd be surprised how creative they get with the word elephant."

Rachel chuckled, pushing off the door frame and making her way to the kitchen. "Let me guess—'E-L-U-F-A-N-T'?"

"That's one of the better attempts," Felicia replied, shaking her head with a smile. "Honestly, I think some of them are doing it on purpose just to keep me entertained."

Opening the fridge, Rachel surveyed the contents with a contemplative hum. "Well, creativity should be encouraged, right? Even if it means you have to decode their hieroglyphics every night."

Felicia's laughter filled the room, a soothing melody that eased some of Rachel's tension. "At this rate, I'll need a degree in cryptology."

Grabbing a few vegetables, Rachel began assembling ingredients on the counter. "How does pasta sound for dinner?"

"Sounds perfect. I'm starving," Felicia said.

Rachel filled a pot with water and set it on the stove. As she chopped tomatoes and garlic, the rhythmic motions gave her a momentary respite from her swirling thoughts. Felicia glanced up periodically, a subtle curiosity clear in her gaze.

"So," Felicia began casually, "how was work today?"

Rachel's hands stilled for a fraction of a second before she resumed chopping. "It was... eventful." She chose her words carefully, unsure of how to broach the subject weighing on her mind.

Felicia put down her red pen, folding her hands atop the stack of papers. "Eventful good or eventful bad?"

"Depends on how you look at it," Rachel replied, avoiding her sister's piercing gaze.

"Actually, I need to catch you up on a few things," she admitted, wiping her hands on a dish towel.

Felicia's expression shifted to one of concern. "What is it?"

Rachel took a deep breath, summoning her courage. "I met with Warren's lawyer a couple of weeks ago... well, actually, Conner and I both did. Warren included me in his will."

Felicia's eyes widened in surprise. "Wait, what? Rachel, that's... unexpected. In what way were you included in his will?"

"I have a guaranteed job at the ranch for at least the next two years," Rachel explained, leaning against the counter. "I'm to continue training the horses, make decisions about new acquisitions. It's all official."

Felicia sat back in her chair, processing the information. "That's incredible. Did Conner inherit the ranch?"

"He did," Rachel nodded. "But there are conditions. We both have to work together... as best we can. If Conner doesn't fulfill his part and live and work the ranch for a year, ownership could transfer to me."

Felicia raised an eyebrow. "Sounds complicated. How did Conner take the news?"

Rachel sighed, turning back to stir the pot on the stove. "He was shocked, maybe a bit frustrated. But honestly, he sounded confident. He's determined to live here and run the ranch."

Felicia watched her sister, "And..."

"And today, Judd and I went with him to pick up Warren's ashes. Conner is going to have a small graveside ceremony after church. Will you come?"

"Of course I will, Rachel."

"We had lunch today at the Bluebird. Missy waited on us," Rachel continued. "I may need your help with her. She is pretty outspoken when in comes to Conner. She really still has a chip on her shoulders.

"I know she does. She loves you and doesn't want to see you hurt again," Felicia said.

Rachel turned to look at her older sister. "She really was rude today with him. I had to pull her aside and have a chat with her. Felicia, this is all so... messy."

"Messy how?" Felicia pressed gently.

"Being around Conner again after all this time," Rachel admitted, her voice barely above a whisper. "It's bringing back a lot of old feelings—feelings I thought were gone."

Felicia rose from the table and moved to her sister's side. "So you still have genuine feelings for him?"

Rachel met her gaze, vulnerability shining in her eyes. "I thought I'd moved on, but seeing him... being around him... it's like the past ten years never happened in a way. I can see how easy it would be just to slide back into where we were... but then the thinking side of my brain kicks in."

Felicia gave her a sympathetic smile. "Well, maybe this is a second chance for friendship that could grow into something more again."

"He's changed. I can see it and I can feel it," Rachel said, shaking her head. "But there's so much hurt between us. I still have an anger deep inside me. I've been trying really hard to push it even further down."

"Do you think you can you forgive him and move on... at least try to be friends," Felicia asked.

Rachel stirred the pasta absently, her mind swirling with memories. "I'm trying. But investing in someone who might leave when things get tough again, I just don't know... Could you trust him again?"

"This isn't about me, but since you asked... yes, I could learn to trust him again. I could forgive him. It would be the moving past the hurt stage that would be hard for me," she said. "You're stronger now. You're a different person now. And maybe he's changed for the better in some ways. You'll never know unless you give it a try. I'd start slow, work on being good friends. I would also ask him his side of the story about why he left. There's always two sides to every story."

"True, but the fact that he left without saying goodbye, that's what hurts the most. I felt like I didn't matter, like I was some whim that could be thrown into the wind. Seriously, Felicia, we were talking about getting married and everything."

"I know," she said. "Personally, I think Conner has some explaining to do. Listen to me, there's always more than one side of a situation.

I'm not saying that Warren lied to you, but he could have left some of the details out. All you know is that they argued and, according to Warren, things got heated and supposedly, Conner ran his mouth and then left."

They settled at the table with bowls of pasta and fresh bread. The simplicity of the meal was a welcome contrast to the complexity of their conversation.

"So, tell me more about Conner," Felicia prompted gently. "What's he like now?"

Rachel took a bite of pasta, gathering her thoughts. "He's... older, of course. He's more mellow. Quiet and thoughtful. He seems like he cares more about others than he does himself. There's a depth to him that wasn't there before. He's seen things, been through a lot, I can sense that. Part of me wonders what happened during those years away."

"Have you asked him?"

"Not yet," Rachel admitted. "I haven't figured out how to ask. And part of me is not sure if I want to know, honestly."

Felicia nodded thoughtfully. "Maybe starting with small talk would help. Find common ground again."

Rachel looked out the window, the twilight casting a serene glow over the fields. "I just don't want to step in too deep. I think I can handle being friends with him again... it certainly would make working with him easier."

"Understandable," Felicia agreed. "You've basically got two choices. One, you continue the way you are, and I imagine you're doing everything possible to avoid him. I can see you going out of your way not to talk to him. Or two, you meet him head on, say let's work this out, let's have an adult conversation and move past all the drama and be friends. Nothing more. Just friends."

Felicia reached across the table and squeezed Rachel's hand gently and continued. "Just take it one day at a time. No need to rush into anything you're not ready for."

Rachel exhaled slowly, her eyes reflecting a mix of pain and nostalgia. "I'll be honest, Felicia, it's been incredibly hard being around him again. We've had a few conversations, and I spoke to him—not with anger, but with sincerity. Over the past few days, I haven't gone out of my way to avoid him. Quite the opposite, actually. But working alongside someone you once loved so deeply, knowing he's just within arm's reach, yet feeling this immense gulf between us—it's unbearable. The love I had for him was profound, but he's also the same person who broke my heart more than I ever thought possible. It feels like this awful, tangled knot inside me. I just can't seem to unravel it."

"I can imagine how overwhelming that must be. Pray about it, Rachel. Opening your heart can only lead to healing."

Rachel sighed, her gaze distant. "I haven't been praying as much as I should. I'm having such a hard time forgiving him."

Felicia gave her an encouraging smile. "Prayer certainly couldn't hurt. Maybe even talk with Pastor Sam. Maybe he can help you find a way to at least start forgiving. Forgiveness would be the first step. And remember, I'm here for you."

"I know you are," Rachel squeezed her sister's hand gratefully. "Boy, I sure miss the days when we were kids. Young and carefree without a worry in the world. Life was so simple then."

"That it was. I agree with you one hundred percent."

Chapter 17

Conner turned Thunder toward home, letting the horse pick up a gentle lope. These early morning rides had become a habit he looked forward to each day. It gave him time to think, enjoy the scenery, and reacquaint himself with different areas of the ranch. The morning air was warm and crisp against his face. As he approached the barn, Conner noticed activity near the mare paddock. Several horses clustered near the fence, showing unusual interest in something beyond his view.

He was just dismounting outside the barn when he heard it—Rachel's voice, tight with urgency: "Help! Whoever's coming in, hurry! I need help!"

Conner's heart lurched at the panic in Rachel's voice. He quickly secured Thunder to the hitching post and sprinted into the barn, boots thundering against the wooden flooring. "Rachel?"

"Here! In Starlight's stall!"

He followed her voice to the last stall on the left, where he found Rachel kneeling beside the pregnant mare they'd all been watching carefully for the past week. The horse was down on her side, sides heaving, clearly distressed.

"She's foaling," Rachel said without looking up, her hands moving with practiced efficiency as she checked the mare. "It's too early... she's not due for another two weeks."

Conner stepped into the stall, his presence causing Starlight to toss her head nervously. "What do you need me to do?"

"Talk to her," Rachel instructed, her voice steady despite the tension in her shoulders. "She's scared."

Conner moved to Starlight's head, speaking in low, soothing tones. "Easy, girl. Easy now. We've got you." The mare's dark eyes rolled toward him, nostrils flaring, but she seemed to calm slightly at his voice.

"The foal's positioned wrong," Rachel said, her face tight with concentration. "I can feel it. We need to turn it before she pushes again, or we could lose them both."

The gravity of her words hit Conner like a physical punch to the gut. He'd seen foals lost before, it was part of ranch life, but the thought of it happening now, on his watch, was unbearable.

"Tell me what you want me to do," he said, and something in his tone made Rachel look up at him. Their eyes met across the stall, and for a moment, the years between them seemed to dissolve. They were just two people united in purpose, trying to save a life.

"I need you to help me position her," Rachel said, all business now. "We need to get her up on her sternum—it'll give me better access. And Conner?" She held his gaze. "Whatever happens, don't let go. If she thrashes, we could both get hurt."

Conner nodded, moving to help Rachel reposition the mare. Starlight was heavy with her foal, and it took both of their strength to get her into position. The mare trembled beneath their hands, sweat darkening her coat.

"Good girl," Rachel murmured, running a practiced hand along the mare's flank. "Now comes the hard part." She glanced at Conner, her face flushed with exertion. "I need to turn the foal. Keep her as still as you can."

Conner positioned himself to brace Starlight's shoulders, murmuring steady reassurances as Rachel worked. The mare's muscles quivered beneath his hands, and he could feel her gathering tension as another contraction approached.

"Easy now, girl," he soothed, though his heart was racing. The barn had grown eerily quiet, as if every creature within sensed the gravity of the moment. Even the morning birds outside the barn seemed to have hushed their songs.

Rachel's face was a mask of concentration as she worked, her movements careful but decisive. "The foal's front leg is bent back," she explained, voice tight with effort. "I need to—there." She shifted position slightly. "Got it. Now we just need..."

Starlight suddenly tensed, a low groan escaping her. "She's going to push," Rachel warned. "Hold her steady!"

Conner threw his weight against the mare's shoulder as she strained, his boots sliding slightly in the straw. Rachel worked quickly, her movements sure despite the pressure of the moment. Sweat beaded on her forehead, and without thinking, Conner reached out with one hand to brush away a strand of hair that had fallen across her face.

The touch was brief, almost unconscious, but he felt Rachel's slight start of surprise. Their eyes met for a fraction of a second before another of Starlight's contractions demanded their full attention.

"The foal's turning," Rachel announced, relief clear in her voice. "Come on, little one. That's it..."

Minutes stretched like hours as they worked together, the air growing thick with tension and shared purpose. Conner held his breath, releasing it only when Rachel would nod or murmur encouragement. Despite the urgency of the situation, he couldn't help but notice how capable she was, how her quiet strength seemed to flow into both the mare and himself.

"There!" Rachel's exclamation was followed by a rush of movement. "Front feet first—that's what we want. Conner, I need you over here now. Quick!"

He moved to her side, and together they guided the foal as it slipped into the world. It was smaller than it should have been, wet and fragile-looking in the early morning light that streamed through the barn windows.

Rachel was already clearing the foal's airways, her movements swift and practiced. For a moment that seemed to stretch into eternity, nothing happened. Then the tiny chest heaved, and a wet cough brought the foal's first breath.

"Thank you, Lord," Rachel whispered. Conner noticed the tears in her eyes as she worked to clean the newborn.

Relief flooded through Conner as the foal struggled to lift its head, its movements weak but determined. Rachel was checking its vitals, her hands moving with gentle efficiency over the spindly legs and small body.

"A filly," she announced softly, a smile breaking across her tired face. "She's small, but she's a fighter."

Starlight had begun to show interest in her offspring, nickering softly as she stretched her neck toward the foal. Rachel guided the mare's movements, ensuring both mother and baby were positioned properly for their first meeting.

Conner watched in wonder as the filly made her first wobbling attempt to stand. His father's voice echoed in his memory: *There's nothing quite like seeing new life come into the world. Reminds you that miracles still happen."*

Rachel glanced up at him. Her face was smudged with dirt and sweat, her hair falling loose from its braid, but there was something luminous about her at that moment, something that made his chest tighten with emotions.

"We need to make sure she nurses," Rachel said, her voice pulling him back to the present. "Can you...?" She swayed slightly as she tried to stand, exhaustion finally catching up with her.

Without thinking, Conner reached out to steady her, and suddenly, she was leaning against him, her back pressed to his chest. For a heartbeat, maybe two. They stayed that way, her weight solid and warm against him, his hands on her shoulders, both of them breathing hard from the morning's exertion.

Rachel stiffened slightly, becoming aware of their position, but fatigue seemed to override her usual careful distance. "Just... give me a minute," she murmured, and Conner tightened his grip slightly.

"Take your time," he said, his voice rougher than he intended. "You did all the hard work."

She shook her head, still not moving away. "Hardly. We helped Starlight together. I couldn't have managed that alone."

The simple honesty in her voice struck him deeper than any accusation could have. Here was Rachel, the woman he'd walked away from, the woman who had every right to hate him, trusting him enough to lean on him, to acknowledge his help.

The moment stretched between them, fragile as spider silk, until a soft rustle of straw brought their attention back to the foal. Rachel straightened slowly, and Conner let his hands fall away from her shoulders, immediately missing the warmth of the contact.

"Look at her," Rachel said softly, watching as the filly made another determined attempt to stand. "Despite everything being against her, she's not giving up."

The sunlight streaming through the barn windows caught the foal's damp coat, turning it to burnished copper. She was small—too small, really—but there was something fierce in her struggles to rise, something that spoke of an untamed will to live.

"She gets that from her mama," Conner said, watching as Starlight nickered encouragement to her baby. "Starlight's a fighter."

Rachel glanced at him. "She really is."

The foal finally gained her feet, wobbling precariously but staying upright. Rachel moved forward to guide her toward Starlight's udder, her hands sure and practiced. "Come on, little one. You need to eat."

Conner watched them, struck by how natural Rachel looked, covered in dirt and straw, completely focused on ensuring this new life got the best possible start. She'd always had this gift, this ability to nurture and heal. It was one of the many things he'd...

He cut the thought off sharply, but not before Rachel caught something in his expression. She tilted her head slightly, studying him with those hazel eyes that had always seen too much.

"What is it?"

"Nothing," he blurted. Then, because he owed her at least this much honesty, "Just... thinking about how good you are at this. At all of it."

Rachel's cheeks colored slightly, but she didn't look away. "It's what I was meant to do. God has a way of leading us where we need to be."

The easy faith in her voice made something twist in Conner's chest. How did she do that? How did she trust so completely in a plan he couldn't even see?

"I should check on Thunder," he said abruptly, needing space from the intensity of the moment. "Will you be okay here?"

Rachel nodded, already turning back to the foal. "We'll be fine. I'll get Judd to help me monitor them when he comes in." She paused, then added quietly, "Thank you, Conner. For being here when I needed you."

The words followed him out of the barn, echoing in his mind as he walked into the morning sunlight. Thunder nickered a greeting from the hitching post, but Conner barely heard it. His thoughts were still in the barn with Rachel, with the miracle they'd just witnessed together.

He glanced back at the barn door, remembering Rachel's whispered prayer of thanks. She had something he'd lost long ago—or maybe never really had. A faith that made her strong, that helped her forgive, that let her see God's hand in the morning light and in new life and in second chances.

Running a hand over his face, Conner tried to shake off the unsettling thoughts. He had a ranch to run, work to do. He couldn't afford to get lost in wondering about faith and forgiveness and the way Rachel's weight had felt against him, solid and real and right.

But as he led Thunder toward the corral, he couldn't quite silence the small voice in his heart that whispered maybe... God wasn't finished with him yet.

Chapter 18

Warren's study was overwhelmingly cluttered. Papers were piled high on every available surface, threatening to cascade to the floor with the slightest provocation. Bookshelves sagged under the weight of countless volumes, their spines cracked and titles faded, some stacked horizontally atop the vertical rows like afterthoughts. Trinkets and knickknacks collected over the years occupied any remaining space, silent witnesses to a life Conner realized he knew very little about.

He let out a low whistle. "Well, Dad, you certainly left me a mess," he muttered under his breath, stepping further inside.

The massive oak desk that dominated the center of the room was buried under a haphazard array of yellowed receipts, unopened letters, and scattered photographs whose edges curled with age.

Conner reached out and picked up a framed picture lying face down among the clutter. He turned it over to reveal a black-and-white photograph of his parents on their wedding day. His mother, Luella, beamed up at Warren, who looked uncharacteristically carefree, a wide grin stretching across his face. Conner felt a tightness in his chest, a mix of longing and regret, tightening like a vise.

"You both really loved each other," he thought, setting the photo gently back on the desk.

He hadn't expected this task to be easy, but the sheer volume of stuff was daunting. Conner rubbed the back of his neck, a nervous habit he hadn't shaken since his rodeo days.

He began sorting through the papers, making piles of what to keep, what to toss, and what to scrutinize later. Bills from years ago mingled with handwritten notes about horse prices and feed suppliers. He found an old map of the ranch, edges frayed and marked with his father's precise handwriting indicating landmarks, grazing rotations and water sources.

As he shuffled through stacks of papers, another leather-bound journal caught his eye. Conner's hand hovered over it, a flicker of hesitation halting his movement.

The stitching along the spine was coming loose in places, and he could see pages stuffed with loose scraps of paper peeking out at odd angles. A part of him feared what he might find within its pages, but a stronger part needed to know.

Conner sank into the old leather armchair, the seat cushion sagging under his weight. He traced the embossed name "Warren Hart" on the cover before taking a deep breath and opening the journal to the first entry.

March 15th

It's been two weeks since I poured the last bottle down the sink. The silence in this house is louder than ever, but the fog is starting to lift. Every day without the bottle is a battle, but it's a fight I need to win. For myself. Maybe even for Conner, if he ever comes back.

Conner blinked, his heart skipping a beat. He read the lines again. His father's words settling heavily on his shoulders. He remembered his father as a man with a glass perpetually in hand, the sharp scent of whiskey or beer on his breath a constant presence in their interactions.

He leaned back, the leather chair creaking in protest. Turning the page, he continued reading.

March 22nd

Ran into Mrs. Carter at the Valley Grocery Store today. She asked about Conner, and I didn't have the heart to tell her we hadn't spoken in a while. Told her he's doing well, out making his mark on the world. Lord, how did it come to this? If only I could take back those words, that darned pride of mine. I miss my boy more than I can bear.

Conner felt a lump forming in his throat. He remembered Mrs. Carter. She used to make the best homemade chicken soup in the valley. The realization that his father had been putting on a brave face, hiding their estrangement from the townsfolk, cut deep.

"Dad..." he trailed off, unsure of what he wanted to say.

He shifted in the chair. He turned to the next entry.

April 5th

Rachel stopped by with a basket of muffins this morning. Said she had extras from baking for some church gathering she was going to. She probably noticed I haven't been eating right. That girl has a way of brightening the darkest days. Reminds me so much of Luella. She sat a spell and talked about the horses. Her laughter fills this empty house and makes me feel a bit better. Not so lonely.

Conner's eyes lingered on Rachel's name. He could almost hear her laugh, that light, musical sound that used to make his heart race when they were younger. Still did, to be honest.

He wondered how many times she'd sat, offering comfort to a lonely old man.

He sighed and rubbed his temples. Conner flipped to another entry, dated a few weeks later.

April 20th

Agreed to a date with Linda Mae—first date since my Luella. Thought maybe it was time. It was a disaster. Spilled coffee on my lap, called her 'Luella' twice, and to top it off, tripped over a darn cat that was on the sidewalk and I didn't see it on the way out of the restaurant. I'm clearly not cut out for this. My heart still belongs to my Luella, and no amount of lonely nights will change that.

Conner couldn't help but chuckle softly. "Classic Dad. Smooth as sandpaper."

He tried to imagine his father on a date, the stern, no-nonsense Warren Hart fumbling through awkward small talk and mishaps. The image was both endearing and heartbreaking.

"Guess you were lonelier than I thought," Conner said.

He leaned forward, elbows resting on his knees, as he stared at the journal. The entries painted a picture of a man he didn't recognize—a man who struggled, who missed his son, who tried in his own way to reach out.

"Why didn't you reach out to me?" he thought. *"Or better yet, why didn't you just come home, Conner"*

But he knew why. The same stubborn pride that kept him away all these years had likely kept his father from reaching out as well. They were more alike than he'd ever wanted to admit.

He flipped through a few more pages, skimming entries about ranch work, weather concerns, and notes on the horses. Then a line caught his eye.

May 1st

I wish I could talk to Conner and tell him the truth. It's weighing heavy on me these last few months. I guess quitting the bottle has me thinking more clearly and remembering things I'd rather not. Conner's down in Texas. He won the grand prize this past weekend.

Conner's brow furrowed. "The truth?" he muttered.

He searched the following pages, but the next few entries were torn out, leaving ragged edges where the pages used to be. His pulse quickened.

"What's this about, Dad?" he thought.

"Conner?"

He looked up, startled. "Rachel, I'm sorry—I didn't hear you come in."

"I just wanted to let you know that Starlight and her foal are doing great. No signs of any problems with either."

"That's good to hear," Conner said, glancing around the room. "I'm just trying to sort through some of this mess in here."

Rachel nodded and pointed at Warren's journal. "Gosh, you'll probably find many of those in here."

"So far, this is only the second one I've found. This one is from several years back," he said, glancing down.

Near the back of the journal, an envelope was stuffed between the pages. Conner pulled it out. It was addressed to him, written in his father's familiar scrawl.

He turned the envelope over and showed it to Rachel. "A letter from Dad."

He opened it, curiosity and dread both mixing within him.

Dear Conner,

If you're reading this, it means I never got the chance to tell you in person. First, I need you to know that I'm sorry. For everything. For the way I treated you, for not being the father you deserved, and for driving you away when all I wanted was to keep you close.

I apologize for drinking so much.

I am so very sorry for those awful last words I spoke to you before you left.

There's something you need to know, something I've carried with me for too long. It concerns your mother and the choices I made after she passed. I wanted to tell you years ago, but I could never find the words or the courage.

Son, your mama didn't pass away in her sleep. She was so distraught and depressed over her cancer diagnosis; she ended her own life. She took too many painkillers on her last day here on earth. I've let you believe for years that she died peacefully in her sleep, but she didn't.

That day, while you were at school, I was out working on the ranch. I knew better. I sensed something was off with your mama that day, but I brushed it off. When I came home to check on her, she was gone. She left me a note telling me she couldn't take living anymore. She feared the pain the doctors had told her was coming would be too much to handle. Your mama said she wanted to go to Heaven with the memory of your smiling face and not one of you crying, broken-hearted, watching her die.

I apologize for lying to you. At the time, I knew you couldn't under-stand the truth of how your mama died because you were so young. But as the years went on, I just never had the guts to tell you the truth. Shoot... I probably should just take this secret to my grave with me, but it just doesn't feel right, you not knowing the truth.

I pray you'll find it in your heart to forgive me one day.

Love, Dad.

Conner stared at the letter, his chest tight as questions swirled in his mind. He slowly extended it toward Rachel, his hand trembling just enough to betray the storm in his heart. His eyes met hers briefly, but he couldn't hold her gaze. He swallowed hard, unsure of what to say.

Rachel took the letter, her fingers brushing his just for a moment before she began to read. Her lips parted as though she might say something, but the words didn't come. When she finally lifted her eyes to him, her expression was unreadable, yet her silence said enough. After a long pause, she finished the letter, folding it carefully before placing it back into the journal, her composure hiding the unspoken questions lingering in her mind.

Rachel moved slowly around the desk, approaching him as though she feared he might pull away or close himself off. She rested her hand lightly on his shoulder, her touch warm and reassuring as her other hand brushed along the edge of the cluttered desk. "Conner, are you okay?" she asked gently, the words full of genuine concern.

Conner sucked in a deep breath, his chest tight as he tried to un-tangle the storm of thoughts swirling in his head. "Yes and no," he said finally, shaking his head and clenching his jaw. "My mom committed suicide." He spat out the word like it was foreign, something that didn't belong in his truth. "That part... that part I'm not okay with. How could I be? But then—I don't know—another part of me tries to think maybe she died on her own terms, you know? She didn't suffer like she thought she would. She didn't have to face the pain the way the doctors told her she would." He glanced down at his hands, frowning deeply. "So, what's right about that? What's wrong? How do you even begin to judge it?"

"There aren't simple answers to questions like that, Conner," she said, her voice still soft but resolute. Her grip on his shoulder tightened briefly, offering what little comfort she could. "I'm so sorry you had to find out like this. You didn't deserve that."

"Me too," Conner muttered, his voice quiet and hoarse. His eyes lifted to hers, full of a raw vulnerability he rarely let anyone see. "What was going through her mind, Rachel? What kind of desperation drives a person to something so... final?" His voice cracked on the last word, and suddenly anger flared brightly in his tone. "And what kind of God just—you know, just lets it happen? Watches someone suffer so much they think dying is better than staying? How... how is that fair at all?!"

Rachel didn't immediately answer, sensing his anger pressing down on him like a heavy yoke. She moved to kneel beside him so she could meet his gaze head-on, her fingers curling gently around his forearm. Her touch was steady and strong, grounding him in a moment when he felt like he might spin out of control. She didn't flinch at his anger, didn't try to soothe it away with empty platitudes. Instead, she let his words hang in the air, giving them the respect they deserved before she spoke.

"I don't know, Conner," she said softly but firmly, her eyes locked on his. "I don't have the answers to those questions. And maybe I never will. But what I do know is that your mama was in pain—deeper pain than she could bear. And sometimes, when people hurt that much, they can't see a way forward." She paused, her voice steady despite the ache that she felt in her chest. "It doesn't make it fair, and it doesn't make it right."

Conner listened, his lips pressed together in a thin line, his jaw taut like steel. He didn't respond right away. Instead, he leaned back in the chair, the worn leather to groaned beneath his weight. His eyes turned toward the ceiling, his thoughts racing too fast for him to catch.

"I always thought..." his voice wavered for a moment, and he cleared his throat harshly, trying to steady it. "I always thought she was the strongest person I ever knew. She was the heart of this place, Rachel. When she was around, everything felt whole. It felt... right." He shifted forward again, leaning his elbows onto his knees, his hands clasped tightly together. "I never saw it. I never saw she was... struggling like that. How could I not have noticed?"

Rachel's heart broke at the pain in his voice, the way the words tumbled out like stones he couldn't carry anymore. "You were a little boy, Conner," she said gently. "It wasn't your responsibility to notice. It wasn't your burden to bear. You couldn't have known."

He scoffed bitterly, shaking his head. "Doesn't make it any easier to swallow, does it? Don't stop me from wishing I could go back and... and just be there for her somehow. From wishing I could have done something—anything—to stop her."

Rachel's hand moved from his arm to cover one of his clenched fists, her touch soft against the tension in his skin. "I think that's part of loving someone, Conner—feeling like you should've been able to fix what hurt them, even when it wasn't something you could control. It's not fair, but it's human. But don't you think she'd want you to remember the good things, too? The laughter, the love, the mornings she made you cinnamon toast or the afternoons she helped you with your homework? Don't let the pain erase the best parts of her you remember."

He nodded slowly, swallowing past the lump in his throat. "I know," he admitted. "I know you're right. But it's hard to see past it right now, Rachel. It's just... this is awful having the memory of your mom tainted like this."

Rachel rose, shifting to sit on the edge of the desk beside him. "You know what I think?" she began, her gaze drifting for a moment to the framed photograph of Warren and Luella on their wedding day. "I think she loved you something fierce, Conner. Fierce enough that she wanted to protect you from her pain, even when it meant leaving this world earlier."

Her words hit him like a gust of wind, cutting through the haze of sorrow and anger that clouded his mind. He leaned forward again, his hands scrubbing over his face in a gesture of exhaustion and frustration. "Yeah," he murmured, his voice muffled behind his hands. "Maybe she thought she was sparing me. And maybe... maybe she was. But it doesn't make it hurt any less, Rachel."

"I know," she replied softly, reaching out to rest a comforting hand on his shoulder. "And it's okay for it to hurt. That means she mattered—to your life, to your heart. Sometimes the people we love most leave behind the deepest scars. But those scars... they're part of who we are. And the love? That stays. Even when they're gone, it stays."

Conner let those words settle into his soul for a moment, filling him with a bittersweet ache. He exhaled slowly, the tension in his shoulders loosening just a fraction. His head dipped forward, his forehead nearly brushing the tops of his knees as he tried to find solid footing amidst the emotional chaos.

"Look," he said, raising back up, his voice low. "This is just another piece of the puzzle with my dad. Another thing in his life that pushed him deeper into the bottle." He glanced up at her, his eyes clouded with emotion. "He loved my mom more than anything. Losing her... it destroyed him for most of his life."

"What do I do with all of this, Rachel?" He continued, "What do I do with knowing that my dad became a new man eventually, a better person, and I wasn't here to enjoy that? What do I do with knowing my mom took her own life?"

Rachel tilted her head slightly, studying him with an expression that was equal parts compassion and determination. "You start by forgiving yourself," she said simply. "And then... maybe you forgive him, too." She gestured toward the journal. "Warren made mistakes—I know he wouldn't argue about that. We all do. Not one person on this earth is perfect. But he loved you, Conner. In his own flawed way, he was trying to make things right."

Conner's brow furrowed as he looked at the journal, and then at the scattered papers that surrounded him. The mess felt less overwhelming now, though no less significant. His father's life was in these piles—the good, the bad, the heartbreak, and the hope. And maybe, just maybe, there was a chance for healing buried in there, too.

He nodded slowly, determination flickering in his eyes. "I think it's about time I try," he said quietly, "because if I don't, I'll end up just like him."

Rachel smiled faintly, the corners of her lips tugging upward in encouragement. "That's all anyone can do, Conner—try," she said.

He nodded again and picked up the journal, flipping through it.

"I have an idea," she said, her voice carefully steady, though her heart was racing.

Conner lifted his head, a guarded look in his deep blue eyes. "What is it?" he asked, his tone low.

"Let's leave all of this—" she gestured vaguely around the room, "—aside for the rest of the day. What's in the past is in the past. We can't change any of it."

Her voice faltered slightly. The sincerity in her tone betrayed the effort it was taking to say those words—to let go, even for a moment. And then, as her hazel eyes flicked up to meet his, she added, with a small but hopeful smile, "It's a gorgeous day outside. Let's saddle up a couple of horses and take a break from... everything."

Conner stood, folding his arms across his chest. For a moment, the tension in his jaw was visible—a silent war waged within him. "What's in the past is in the past," he echoed slowly, his voice rough with disbelief. He leaned forward, closing the space between. "Is that all it takes? Just say it, and that's it? You can forget about everything? About me leaving? About..." His voice cracked before he could finish, and he turned his head away, swallowing hard.

Rachel's breath hitched, but she didn't look away. She couldn't—it felt too important. "No," she admitted quietly, her voice trembling with an edge of vulnerability she'd long avoided around him. "It's not that easy, Conner. It's not... easy at all."

He stilled, his blue eyes searching hers, waiting for her to continue. She hesitated, something in her gaze softening, despite the years of hurt lodged between them.

"But maybe we could start small," she added finally, her voice barely above a whisper. "Just... for today. Let's just try to breathe for a little while. Leave what we can't fix behind, if only for a moment."

"And then what, Rachel?" he pressed, his voice softer now, loaded with need and unspoken regret. "When the day ends, what happens then?"

Rachel's lips parted, but her answer didn't come right away. She dropped her gaze, her fingers brushing over the smooth edge of the desk. After a long pause, something flickering in her expression—resolve, maybe, or hope dimmed by uncertainty. When she finally spoke, her voice was steady, even if her emotions weren't entirely so.

"For now," she said simply, raising her eyes to his again. A trace of something deeper—something long-buried—lingered in her gaze. "Let's just start there and see where it leads."

Conner stood motionless, caught between holding on to his guilt and reaching for the sliver of grace she was offering. When he finally nodded, it wasn't in surrender, not completely—it was cautious, unsure, but it was a start. And somehow, that felt like everything.

Chapter 19

Conner and Rachel led their saddled horses outside the barn. The air was thick with the sweet scent of fresh-cut hay from the nearby fields, and a gentle breeze rustled through the air.

"So, where to?" Conner asked, adjusting his stirrup before swinging up onto his horse's back. He settled into the saddle, the leather creaking beneath him.

Rachel mounted her horse, a hint of mischief dancing in her hazel eyes as she gathered her reins. "Follow me," she said, flashing him a smile that stirred something deep in his chest—a memory of younger, simpler days.

Before he could respond, she nudged her horse forward, breaking into a canter that quickly became a gallop. Her blonde hair whipped behind her as she raced across the south pasture, leaving him no choice but to follow.

Conner urged his horse after her, feeling a rush of exhilaration as they thundered across the open ground. The wind rushed past his face, and for a moment, he felt lighter, freer.

They rode past the weathered fence posts marking the southern boundary of the ranch, past the old spruce grove where horses often sought shade, and toward the distant silhouette of the Sapphire Mountains. Rachel's laughter floated back to him on the wind, pure and uninhibited, and he smiled despite everything.

He caught up to her as the terrain began to roll more dramatically, their horses falling into an easy stride side by side. The mountains loomed closer now, their peaks touched with the last remnants of snow, their slopes carpeted in deep green pine forests.

"I'd almost forgotten what this feels like," Conner said, his voice carrying a note of wonder.

Rachel glanced over at him, her cheeks flushed from the ride. "What? The riding or the freedom?"

"Both, maybe." He adjusted his grip on the reins, studying the familiar landscape that somehow looked different after so many years away. "Everything's the same, but different, you know?"

She nodded, understanding in her eyes. "Sometimes the things that change the most are the ones we can't see."

They rode in companionable silence as the path narrowed, winding its way toward a bend in the river where the water tumbled over smooth rocks. The sound of rushing water grew louder, mixing with the gentle clop of hooves and the occasional call of a red-tailed hawk circling overhead.

Rachel guided them to a small clearing beneath a stand of aspens, their silver-white trunks gleaming in the late afternoon light. She dismounted smoothly, leading her horse to a low-hanging branch. "Remember this spot?" she asked, glancing over her shoulder as she secured her reins.

Conner's heart skipped a beat as recognition dawned. Of course, he remembered. This was their spot—had been their spot—back before everything fell apart. He slid from his saddle, memories washing over him like the river's current below.

"Yeah," he said softly, tethering his horse. "I remember."

Rachel was already moving toward a narrow trail that snaked up the rocky embankment, her boots finding footholds with practiced ease. Conner followed, memories flickering through his mind with each step. The path had changed little—still steep in places, still requiring careful attention, but somehow feeling shorter than it had in his memory.

The trail opened onto a natural clearing where several flat rocks jutted out over the river like nature's own viewing platform. The water below rushed past in a constant rhythm, creating swirling eddies around partially submerged boulders. Late afternoon sunlight filtered through the canopy above, casting dappled shadows that danced across the ground.

Rachel settled onto one of the larger rocks, pulling off her boots and socks. "Remember how we used to come up here in the summer?" she asked, rolling up her jeans. "The water was always so cold, but we'd stay for hours, anyway."

Conner watched as she dipped her feet into the clear water, her slight intake of breath at the temperature making him smile. He lowered himself onto the rock beside her, leaving enough space between them to feel proper, but close enough to catch the faint scent of her shampoo on the breeze.

"I remember," he said, removing his boots and socks. "You used to bring those peanut butter cookies your mom made."

"And you'd try to skip stones across the rapids," Rachel added, a gentle laugh escaping her. "Even though I kept telling you, it wouldn't work with the current so strong."

"Hey, I managed it a few times," he protested, but he was smiling too as he submerged his feet in the cold water.

"Pure luck," she teased, then grew quieter. "Remember that time we came up here after your first rodeo win? You were so excited you could barely sit still."

Conner's smile faded slightly. "Yeah. Thought I was invincible back then." He picked up a small stone, turning it over in his hands. "Funny how things turn out."

Rachel was silent for a moment, and he could feel her gaze on him. When he glanced over, he saw the hesitation in her expression, the way she seemed to be contemplating her next words carefully.

"What is it?" he asked. "I can practically hear your mind turning."

She drew in a deep breath, her feet making small ripples in the water below. "Tell me about it, Conner," she said finally, her voice gentle but firm. "Tell me about the rodeo life. About what happened after you left. About the accident and the year after, when nobody knew where you were or if you were even alive."

Conner's fingers tightened around the stone in his hand. He'd known this conversation was coming—had dreaded it, really—but sitting here in this place that held so many innocent memories, he wanted to answer.

Conner stared at the rushing water below, gathering his thoughts. The stone in his hand was smooth, worn down by years of river current—not unlike how his own rough edges had been worn away by time and pain.

"At first, it was everything I dreamed it would be," he began, his voice low but steady. "The rush of adrenaline, the roar of the crowd, the feeling that I was finally becoming somebody important." He tossed the stone into the water, watching it disappear beneath the surface. "Won my first big competition in Texas. Used the prize money to buy a truck that was way too expensive, but I didn't care. I was riding high—literally and figuratively."

Rachel listened quietly, her eyes on his profile as he spoke.

"But success..." he shook his head, "it has a way of making you believe your own hype. I started taking bigger risks, ignoring advice from older riders. Started drinking too much, partying too hard. Thought I was untouchable."

"When did things start to change?" Rachel asked softly.

Conner's jaw tightened. "About eight years in. I was at a competition in Wyoming. There was this bull—meanest thing I'd ever seen. Everyone told me not to ride him. Said he was too unpredictable, too dangerous. But I was..." he paused, shame coloring his voice, "I was drunk. Not falling-down drunk, but enough that my judgment was shot. I insisted on riding him, anyway."

He could feel Rachel tense beside him, knowing what was coming.

"Eight seconds," he continued, his voice rough. "That's all I needed to stay on. I made it to six before everything went wrong. Bull threw me hard, but instead of rolling clear, I got tangled in the rope. Dragged me across the arena before anyone could get to me. By the time they did..." He unconsciously touched his shoulder where the scars still marked his skin. "Well, let's just say I'm lucky to be walking."

"How bad was it?" Rachel asked, her voice barely above a whisper.

"Bad enough. Multiple surgeries over the span of a year on my shoulder, leg, and back. Physical therapy to learn to walk again, then I had to learn to move in ways to ease pain. Doctors said I'd never ride professionally again." He laughed, but there was no humor in it. "Funny thing is, that wasn't even the worst part. The worst part was realizing that everything I'd built my life around—my entire identity—was gone in six seconds."

Rachel's hand moved as if to reach for him, but she pulled it back. "And after that? That year, when no one knew where you were?"

Conner's expression darkened. "I spiraled. I wanted to come back here, but I couldn't face coming back as a failure. Couldn't face telling Dad he was right all along. So I disappeared. Ended up in some cheap motel in New Mexico, drinking myself numb most days. I was hooked on pain pills for a while too—anything to dull the pain, physical and otherwise. Until my doctors cut me off and wouldn't refill me prescription. I can honestly say they helped save my life by telling me no."

He glanced at Rachel, expecting to see judgment in her eyes, but found only compassion. It made his chest ache.

"What made you stop drinking?" she asked quietly.

Conner drew in a deep breath, the scent of pine and river water filling his lungs. The late afternoon sun had dipped lower, casting long shadows across the water.

"Rock bottom came in a dirty bathroom in Albuquerque," he said, his voice tight. "I'd been on a three-day bender, mixing whatever I could get my hands on. Woke up on the floor, couldn't remember how I got there. Looked in the mirror and didn't recognize the person staring back at me." He swallowed hard. "That's when I knew—if I didn't change something, I was going to die there, alone in some nameless motel."

Rachel's hand moved again, and this time she didn't pull back. Her fingers brushed his arm, light as a whisper but grounding somehow.

"So I checked myself into rehab," he continued. "Spent six months getting clean, learning how to live with the pain—both kinds. Then another six months working odd jobs, trying to piece myself back together." He looked down at where Rachel's hand rested on his arm. "Never thought I'd end up back here under these circumstances, though."

"But you did," Rachel said softly. "Maybe that means something."

Conner glanced at her. "Like what?"

"Like maybe God had a plan, even when you couldn't see it." Her voice was gentle, careful—like she was afraid of pushing too hard.

He felt a familiar resistance rise at the mention of God, but something in her expression made him pause. "You really believe that, don't you? That there's some divine plan in all this mess?"

Rachel's eyes met his, steady and sure. "I do. I've seen it in my own life, in your father's life—"

"Dad?" Conner interrupted, surprised.

She nodded. "After you left, when he quit drinking... it wasn't just about getting sober. He found faith, Conner. Real, transformative faith. It changed him."

Conner absorbed this, thinking about the journal entries he'd read earlier. "And you think... what? That God's got some redemption story planned for me too?"

"I think," Rachel said carefully, "that God doesn't waste anything—not even our mistakes. Sometimes the longest trails lead us exactly where we need to be."

The water continued its endless journey below them, constant and unchanging. Conner watched a leaf spiral past in the current, thinking about paths and choices and second chances.

"I don't know if I can believe like you do, Rachel," he admitted finally. "I've done too much, hurt too many people—" his voice caught slightly, "—hurt you."

Rachel's fingers tightened slightly on his arm. "Faith isn't about being perfect, Conner. It's about being willing to take the first step, even when you can't see the whole path."

As the sun dipped lower behind the mountains, casting the valley in soft golden light, Conner wondered if maybe she was right. But the thought scared him almost as much as it gave him hope.

"We should probably head back," Rachel said, withdrawing her hand. "It'll be dark soon."

Conner nodded, but neither of them moved immediately. The moment felt fragile somehow, like a soap bubble that might burst if disturbed too quickly.

Rachel stood after putting on her socks and boots. As she turned toward the trail, Conner found his voice again.

"Rachel?"

She paused, looking back at him. The fading sunlight caught in her hair, creating a soft halo effect that made his heart skip.

"Thank you," he said simply. "For listening. For not judging. For..." he gestured vaguely at the clearing, "...for sharing this place with me again."

A small smile touched her lips, gentle and genuine. She held out her hand to him as she said, "Sometimes, we all need a reminder of who we used to be to figure out who we want to become."

Chapter 20

Conner leaned against the rough bark of the cottonwood tree, his father's bronze urn sitting beside him on a weathered wooden bench. The Montana landscape around him was painted in rich hues of green, wildflowers of various colors swayed in the breeze, but he barely noticed the surrounding beauty. His attention was focused on the freshly dug grave nearby, its dark earth a stark reminder of what he'd lost, and what he'd thrown away years ago.

He picked up the urn, its weight substantial in his hands. Strange how something so heavy could contain what remained of a man who'd once seemed larger than life. Warren Hart had been many things, stubborn, hard-drinking, difficult to please, but never small. Not until the end, when Conner hadn't been there to see him change, to witness his transformation into the man everyone else seemed to have known.

The sound of hoofbeats drew his attention. Through the trees, he caught glimpses of riders approaching—Judd, Will, and Levi leading the way. Behind them, a stream of vehicles followed slowly, making their way over the uneven ground. Conner straightened, confusion creasing his brow. He'd expected a small, private service, just the ranch hands, Rachel and Minnie. But this...

He watched as the riders dismounted. He watched as people, some familiar, exited their vehicles.

Pastor Sam reached him first, his kind face creased with sympathy. "Conner," he said warmly, extending his hand. "I hope you don't mind that we spread the word about Warren's service."

"Who are all these people?" Conner asked, watching as more vehicles parked and people began making their way toward the cemetery.

"These are your father's friends, his brothers, and sisters in Christ," Pastor Sam explained. "They wanted to see him off and stand here for you. That's community, son. These people are here for you and your dad."

Conner swallowed hard, overwhelmed by the steady stream of people filing through the cemetery gate, others standing around him near the cottonwoods. Some faces he recognized, others were complete strangers, yet they all shared the same look of quiet respect.

Movement near the gate caught his eye, and his breath caught in his throat. Rachel stood there, elegant in a fitted black dress that hugged her curves, her honey-blonde hair swept up in a neat chignon. The sight of her made his heart race, stirring emotions he'd been trying to keep buried.

"Conner." Judd's gruff voice pulled his attention away from Rachel. The foreman and the other ranch hands approached, carrying something between them—a small, beautifully crafted oak coffin.

"What's this?" Conner asked, his voice rough with emotion.

Judd cleared his throat. "I hope you don't mind. Levi, Will, and I... we wanted him laid to rest proper, with something made by our hands."

Conner stared at the coffin, noting the careful joinery, the hand-rubbed finish that gleamed in the sunlight. "It's beautiful. I don't know what to say."

"No worries," Judd said quietly, setting a firm hand on Conner's shoulder.

Pastor Sam entered the cemetery, taking his place near the grave. Conner followed. The crowd gathered close, forming a respectful semicircle. Conner scanned their faces—the elderly couple who owned the hardware store, several ranchers he remembered from his youth, women, and men who must have known his father from church. Each face told a story of connection, of relationship, of the life his father had built while Conner was running from his own.

"We gather today," Pastor Sam began, his voice carrying clearly across the hushed crowd, "to lay to rest our brother in Christ, Warren Hart. A man who knew the transformative power of God's grace, who showed us all that it's never too late to change, to seek forgiveness, to begin again."

Conner's throat tightened. He thought of the father he'd known, angry, bitter, drowning his demons in whiskey. How had that man become someone worthy of such words?

"Warren's journey wasn't easy," Pastor Sam continued. "He faced his failures, his mistakes, his broken relationships with courage and humility. He found faith despite his struggles. And in doing so, he showed us all what amazing grace truly means."

Rachel stood across the grave from Conner, her eyes fixed on Pastor Sam. Conner could see the shimmer of tears threatening to fall. This woman had stood by his father, unwavering. The thought made his chest ache with regret for all he'd missed.

With reverent care, Conner placed his father's urn inside the hand-crafted oak coffin. His fingers lingered on the smooth wood for a moment before Judd and Will carefully lowered it into the grave. The sound of it settling into place seemed to echo in his chest.

Pastor Sam offered a final prayer, his words drifting up through the cottonwood leaves like incense. When he finished, Judd handed Conner a shovel.

Conner stared at the dark earth piled beside the grave. This was it, the final goodbye he'd never gotten to say in person. His hands tightened on the wooden handle as he stepped forward. The first shovelful of dirt fell with a hollow sound that seemed to reverberate through his bones.

He passed the shovel to Judd, who repeated the gesture with quiet dignity. One by one, the ranch hands and townspeople took their turns, each scoop of earth a testament to Warren Hart's impact on their lives. Some murmured quiet prayers, others simply nodded in respect.

When Rachel stepped forward, Conner couldn't take his eyes off her. She moved with grace, even in this somber task, her face composed but her eyes bright with emotion. After placing her portion of earth in the grave, she handed the shovel to Minnie and turned toward him.

Their eyes met across the space. A tender moment passed between them. Rachel moved to stand beside him, close enough that he could smell her light perfume. Without thinking, Conner reached for her hand.

Her fingers were cool against his. She didn't pull away. Instead, her grip tightened slightly, offering the comfort he knew he didn't deserve, but desperately needed.

They stood together as the last of the earth was placed, watching the grave slowly fill. The late afternoon sun filtered through the cottonwood leaves, casting dappled shadows that danced across the fresh mound of soil.

"Thank you all for coming," Conner said, his voice rough with emotion. "I... I had no idea my father had so many friends and people that cared about him."

"He was loved," Rachel said softly beside him. "He was a good man."

Conner's grip on her hand tightened fractionally. "I wish I'd gotten to know him better."

"Thank you for coming," he murmured, finally turning to look at her fully.

Rachel met his gaze steadily. "He mattered to me. And..." she paused, something vulnerable flickering in her eyes, "you matter too, Conner. That's never fully gone away."

"Everyone," Pastor Sam said. The crowd hushed to silence as the Pastor spoke. He turned his attention to Conner and said. "Conner, the church members and community have prepared a luncheon for you and everyone here to celebrate Warren's life. I'd like to welcome you to join us at the church."

Rachel squeezed his hand, and all Conner could do was nod his head in response.

Chapter 21

Conner spotted Felicia and Missy making their way toward them. The Nolan sisters moved with the same fluid grace as Rachel, though Missy's determined stride contrasted with Felicia's gentler approach.

"Hey Conner," Felicia said, her smile warm and genuine. "It's been a long time. Good to see you."

He nodded, surprised by the lack of judgment in her tone. "Thanks for coming."

Missy, whom he'd expected to be cold, simply said, "This is a good thing you did for your daddy, Conner. It was a beautiful service."

Rachel's fingers squeezed his before she let go. "Felicia drove us here," she said, looking up at him with those expressive eyes. "Why don't you ride with us to the church?"

The invitation surprised him. "I'd appreciate that."

The walk to Felicia's car was quiet, except for the sounds of car doors opening and closing as others prepared to leave. Conner walked beside Rachel, while Felicia and Missy led the way.

Rachel settled in beside him in the back seat, close enough that he could feel the warmth of her presence, yet far enough to maintain a respectable distance.

As Felicia navigated the winding road toward town, Conner stared out the window at the passing Montana landscape. The Sapphire Mountains rose in the distance, their peaks touched by wispy clouds, while closer, the summer wildflowers dotted the rolling hills with splashes of purple, pink, and gold.

"I still can't believe how many people came," he said.

"Your father touched many lives after he found faith," Rachel replied.

From the driver's seat, Felicia nodded. "He sponsored my classroom's reading program for the last three years. He made sure every child had books of their own to keep."

"That doesn't sound like the man I knew," Conner admitted, his voice rough with emotion. "Thank you for telling me that. I am shocked each day to learn more about the man my dad became. It just baffles me."

"His journey was remarkable to witness. He changed me in many ways as well. I enjoyed sitting with him and studying bible verses." Missy said from the passenger seat, her tone gentle.

He glanced at Rachel, finding her watching him with understanding in her eyes. The same understanding he'd seen when she'd stood beside him at the grave.

The Riverbend Valley Community Church came into view, its white steeple rising against the Montana sky. Felicia pulled into the parking lot, which was already filling with cars and trucks from the funeral.

Conner stepped out of the car. The church had changed little in the decade he'd been gone—same white clapboard siding, the same wooden steps leading to the double doors. He stood frozen for a moment, an unexpected memory washing over him.

He was seven years old again, standing on these same steps in his Sunday best, his mother's hand in his on Easter. The last Easter she was alive. His father's large hand held his other hand, steadying him as they climbed the stairs. The memory was so vivid he could almost hear his mother's gentle laugh, feel his father's calloused palm against his.

"Conner?" Rachel's soft voice drew him back to the present. She stood beside him, concern etched in her features. "You okay?"

He swallowed hard. "Just... remembering."

Understanding flickered in her eyes. She touched his arm gently. "Come on. There are many people who want to share their memories of your father with you."

The community hall behind the church was already buzzing with activity when they entered. The large room held long tables covered in checkered clothes, some lining the walls, laden with dishes brought by what seemed like half the county. The scent of fried chicken, fresh biscuits, and various casseroles filled the air.

More people than he'd seen at the graveside were here, their conversations creating an invigorating hum that filled the space. Rather than the scrutiny or judgment he'd expected, he was met with sympathetic smiles and quiet nods of acknowledgment.

Mrs. Kaufman, who'd taught him in third grade, approached first. Her hair had gone completely white, but her eyes were as kind as he remembered. "Conner Hart," she said warmly, reaching for his hands. "Your father was so proud when you started riding rodeo. He kept me updated on all your accomplishments."

The revelation stunned him. "He did?"

"Oh yes. He'd tell me all about your latest win, where you were, even after—" She caught herself, squeezing his hands. "Well... after your accident, he lost track of you... but he continued to share memories of you with me. Talked all the time about how proud he was of you. He loved you, dear. That never changed."

Others came forward—ranchers who'd known his father, church members who shared stories of Warren's transformation, women who'd brought food when he was very sick near the end.

He caught glimpses of Rachel moving through the crowd, helping other women set up the food tables. She moved with a beautiful ease, and it was difficult to keep his eyes from lingering continually on her while trying to pay attention to whomever came to greet him and share kind words and stories.

"If I could have everyone's attention," Pastor Sam's voice carried over the crowd. "Before we share this wonderful meal together, I'd like to ask Conner to step forward and lead us in the line, and then I'll say grace."

Conner felt a moment of panic, but Judd appeared at his elbow. "Come on, boss," the foreman said with a slight grin. "Can't keep these hungry folks waiting."

A ripple of gentle laughter moved through the crowd. Rachel appeared beside him, followed by Minnie and the other ranch hands. The simple act of them gathering around him, supporting him without words, made his throat tight. They stood as a group in front of the Pastor. The congregation quieted as he raised his hands slightly, a gesture that seemed to invite everyone into the moment.

"Let us bow our heads," Sam said, his voice calm and steady, carrying across the hall. "Lord, we thank You for the life of our brother, Warren Hart—a man who showed us the beauty of redemption and the power of Your grace. We ask that You bless this food we are about to share, the hands that prepared it, and the community that has gathered here today. May Your love comfort us in our sorrow and remind us that even in the valley of mourning, Your light leads us forward. Amen."

A chorus of "Amens" followed, and Conner opened his eyes to find the room gazing at him expectantly. Rachel nudged him gently with her elbow. "Time to lead the way," she whispered, her tone encouraging.

Conner swallowed his lingering nerves and stepped forward, a palpable mix of gratitude and vulnerability coursing through him. The crowd parted slightly, giving him a path to the long tables laden with food. He glanced over his shoulder at Rachel, Minnie, Judd, and the other ranch hands who fell in step behind him. It was such a simple thing—leading the line—but for Conner; it felt like the first significant step toward something like belonging.

Though the smells of the freshly prepared food tugged at his appetite, he found himself distracted by the atmosphere. This wasn't just a meal; it was a reflection of everything he'd forgotten about this town, the way neighbors came together in good times and bad, their generosity woven into every casserole dish and basket of homemade biscuits.

He paused at the end of the buffet line, plate in hand, scanning the room for a seating spot. Rachel caught his hesitation. "Follow me."

They walked toward a round table in the corner, and the ranch hands followed behind them.

Judd pulled out a chair. "Have a seat, boss."

Conner smirked slightly at the gruff yet good-natured gesture, muttering a quiet "thanks" as he sat down. Rachel offered him a small smile before turning her attention to Minnie, who was already pointing out which dishes she suspected had come from the best cooks in town.

As the meal continued, lighthearted conversation buzzed around the table. Levi leaned over, pointing his fork at the fried chicken on Conner's plate. "That came from Mrs. Cooper's kitchen. Trust me, you'll never find anything better this side of the valley."

"She must've really liked dad. It's a lot of work to fry chicken," Conner said. He bit into the chicken, savoring the perfectly seasoned crunch. He glanced at Levi. "You weren't kidding."

The table chuckled, and Minnie added, "If Mrs. Cooper shows up with food, it's her way of saying she cares. Otherwise, she just sends a nice card."

"You sure you don't wanna fill the lead volunteer role that's open for the kitchen crew, Minnie?" Rachel teased with a playful nudge. "You seem to know everyone's secrets."

"And I've got ears in every corner of this valley," Minnie replied, tipping her coffee cup toward Rachel with a grin. "You'd be surprised at what I hear during bible study group at church."

The chatter continued, and Conner was easing into the rhythm of it. Although he occasionally caught the curious eyes of other attendees or heard the quiet hum of conversation about his return, he didn't feel the weight of judgment he'd expected. Instead, the room buzzed with genuine welcome, the community's acceptance palpable in the simple act of sharing a meal.

At some point, Conner's attention drifted back to Rachel. She was sitting beside him, engaged with Levi and Will in a conversation about the ranch's yearling horses. Her eyes sparkled with the ease of the moment, and her soft laugh seemed to light up the corner of the hall where they sat. He was struck by how natural she seemed here—how her presence had the power to anchor everyone around her, just as it had anchored him earlier that day.

"You're staring," Minnie whispered in a singsong voice, leaning across the table just enough for Conner to hear.

Startled, Conner blinked and glanced down at his plate. "I'm not staring," he muttered under his breath.

"If you say so," Minnie said with a knowing smirk.

Conner decided it was safer to focus on his food for a while, though he couldn't entirely suppress the thought that Minnie might be right. Rachel had a way of drawing his attention without even trying. She always had.

As the meal wound down, Pastor Sam moved through the room, stopping at each table to speak with the guests. When he reached theirs, he addressed Conner directly.

"I've been meaning to thank you for coming to the luncheon," Pastor Sam said, resting a hand on Conner's shoulder. "It would've meant a lot to your father."

Conner met the pastor's steady gaze. "Thank you for including me... for having this celebration. I'm sure dad would have appreciated this."

Pastor Sam nodded, his expression compassionate. "Don't let your regret blind you to the blessings that are still ahead, son."

Conner's throat tightened at the pastor's words, but he managed a nod. "Thanks, Pastor."

The gathering began to wind down, people trickling out of the hall with leftovers in hand and kind words shared as final reflections on the day. Through it all, Conner felt a tentative but growing sense of connection.

Chapter 22

Rachel leaned against the barn, watching the morning light spill across the land as she waited for Conner. Six teens from a church youth group in the next town over would arrive in less than two hours, and everything needed to be perfect.

"Morning." Conner's deep voice startled Rachel from her thoughts. He stood a few feet away, two steaming coffee mugs in hand. "Thought you might need this."

Rachel accepted the offered mug. Their fingers brushed in the exchange. "Thanks." She took a sip, surprised to find it exactly how she liked it—splash of cream, a dab of sugar. That he remembered after all these years made something flutter in her chest.

"So," Conner said, leaning against the barn door frame. "What's first on the agenda?"

Rachel watched him over the rim of her mug. He looked different today, more settled somehow, like yesterday's memorial luncheon had brightened his spirits. The community's response seemed to have touched something in him, though she knew he was still processing it all.

"We need to choose six horses for the youth clinic," she said. "Ones with the right temperament for teens. Then we'll need to give them a lite groom, check all the tack, and set up the corral."

Conner nodded, his blue eyes scanning the barn interior. "Any horses in particular you're thinking of?"

"I was thinking of Maple, Dusty, and Scout for sure. They're our most reliable with younger riders. Maybe Lightning too. Despite his name, he's actually quite gentle."

A small smile tugged at Conner's lips. "Lightning? Let me guess—Dad named him?"

"Actually, that was me," Rachel admitted, feeling her cheeks warm slightly. "He was born during a big thunderstorm two springs ago. Your father thought it was fitting."

The mention of Warren brought a thoughtful look to Conner's face.

"Whose idea were these youth group clinics? I don't remember anything like this before?" Conner asked.

"Your dad's. He came to me one day and asked my opinion about it. The idea grew from there. And you know what? Your dad loved these clinics and what they came to be. Once a month, the youths come and just enjoy learning about the horses, learning to care for them, learning to ride and strengthening their riding skills. Your dad got such a kick out of the teens."

Their eyes met, and for a moment, Rachel felt that old, familiar connection spark between them.

Conner cleared his throat and stepped back slightly.

"I'd love to have witnessed that. It's hard for me to imagine, but I'll take your word on it," he said, finishing his coffee. "Let's get started. Those horses won't groom themselves."

Rachel watched him head toward the stalls. She couldn't help but notice how naturally he moved in the barn now, so different from his uncertain steps when he'd first returned. Maybe, she thought, they were all changing and moving forward in their own ways.

The next hour passed in a comfortable rhythm as Rachel and Conner worked together, preparing the horses. She stole glances at him when he wasn't looking, noting how gentle he was with each animal, how his muscular hands moved with careful precision as he checked hooves and brushed coats.

"You haven't lost your touch," she observed, watching him expertly detangle Lightning's mane.

Conner paused, a flash of something vulnerable crossing his face. "Funny how some things stay with you, even when you try to leave them behind."

Rachel understood he wasn't just talking about handling horses. She focused on adjusting Scout's saddle, giving herself a moment to steady her voice. "Sometimes the things we try to leave behind are the very things God wants us to come back to."

She heard Conner's soft exhale, but didn't push further. Since their time sitting by the river the other day, she'd noticed him listening more intently whenever faith was mentioned, though he still held himself apart from it.

"Rachel?" His voice was hesitant. "How did you... how did you help Dad find his faith?"

The question surprised her. She turned to face him, finding his blue eyes fixed on her with genuine curiosity.

"I didn't, not really," she said carefully. "I just... I was there for him. After you left, he started drinking even more. Then the morning I found him in the barn passed out, I never let up on him about it," She paused, remembering that difficult time. "I invited him to church continually. He refused at first, but I never gave up. Honestly, your dad did all the hard work. He allowed faith to find him again."

Conner's hands had stilled on Lightning's mane. "Just like that?"

"No, not just like that. It was a process. He struggled, fought it sometimes. Said some harsh things. But he came around. He started coming to church with me. Started attending Bible study with Pastor Sam. Conner, it was honestly a miracle I'm glad I witnessed." Rachel smiled at the memory. "Your father was quite the theologian by the end. He loved debating scripture with anyone who'd engage him."

A sad smile touched Conner's lips. "Sounds like Dad. Always had to have the last word."

"Oh, he did... that's for sure. He changed so much, Conner. Really changed. You would have been so proud of him. Started sponsoring programs at church, helping families in need. Started sponsoring programs at the schools in the area." She met his gaze. "The man you knew and the man he became... they were different people."

"Like the father in the prodigal son's story," Conner said quietly, surprising her with the biblical reference.

"You remember that parable?"

He nodded, returning his attention to Lightning's mane. "Mom used to read it to me. Funny how it hits different now."

Before Rachel could respond, the sound of approaching vehicles drew their attention. Through the barn doors, they could see several cars pulling up, right on schedule.

"They're here," Rachel said. "Ready?"

Conner straightened, brushing his hands on his jeans. For a moment, uncertainty flickered across his face, but then he squared his shoulders. "Ready as I'll ever be."

Rachel touched his arm as she passed. "You'll do fine. Just be yourself."

She headed toward the barn doors, aware of Conner falling into step beside her. As they stepped into the morning sunlight, Rachel sent up a silent prayer of thanks for second chances and the mysterious ways God worked to bring people home.

Six teenagers climbed out of the cars, their nervous energy palpable as they gathered near the barn entrance. Rachel recognized most of them from past clinics—the Anderson twins, Sarah and Matt, both fifteen; Tommy Peterson, the church secretary's sixteen-year-old son; Lisa Martinez, who sang in the county youth choir; and two others she knew by sight but not by name.

"Welcome back to Gold Star Ranch," Rachel called out warmly. "I'm Rachel Nolan, and this is Conner Hart. We'll both be working with you today."

The teens murmured their hellos, some shuffling their feet in the dirt, others casting curious glances at Conner. Rachel noticed Tommy Peterson's eyes widen with recognition.

"Wait—Conner Hart? The bull rider?" Tommy asked, excitement breaking through his initial shyness. "My dad has some old rodeo programs with your name in them!"

Rachel felt Conner tense slightly beside her, but was impressed when he managed a genuine smile. "That was a lifetime ago," he said. "Today, we're focusing on something a lot safer than bull riding."

"Although," Rachel added, seeing an opportunity to build bridges, "Mr. Hart's experience makes him particularly qualified to teach you about staying balanced in the saddle."

The teens seemed to relax a bit at this exchange, and Rachel guided them toward the barn. "First things first. Let's review some basic safety rules, and then we'll introduce you to your horses for today."

As they entered the barn, the familiar sounds and smells seemed to both excite and intimidate the young visitors. Rachel noticed how Lisa Martinez hung back slightly, her eyes wide as she looked at the horses.

"Scared of horses?" Conner asked quietly, falling into step beside Lisa.

The girl nodded, blushing. "I get nervous sometimes."

"Would you like to meet the gentlest horse in Montana?" Conner gestured toward Lightning, whose peaceful demeanor belied his dramatic name.

Rachel watched as Conner guided Lisa toward Lightning's stall, his voice low and encouraging. "Here's the thing about horses," he was saying. "They can sense when you're nervous. But they can also sense when you're trying to be brave."

Something warm bloomed in Rachel's chest as she observed Conner with the teenager. This was a side of him she enjoyed getting to know again—patient, gentle, understanding. It reminded her of the way Warren had been in his later years, always ready with a kind word for those who needed it.

"Miss Nolan?" Sarah Anderson's voice pulled Rachel's attention back to the group. "Which horse will I be riding?"

Rachel directed her focus to the task at hand, but throughout the morning, she found her gaze repeatedly drawn to Conner as he worked with the teens. He seemed to have an instinct for knowing which ones needed extra encouragement and which ones needed their enthusiasm, tempered with caution.

The morning progressed smoothly until Matt Anderson's hat went flying in a gust of wind, startling Dusty and causing a moment of chaos. Rachel's heart jumped as the horse side-stepped nervously, but before she could react, Conner was there.

"Easy, easy," his voice carried across the corral, steady and calm. He caught Dusty's reins, speaking softly to both horse and rider. "You're alright, Matt. Just sit deep and breathe. That's it."

Rachel watched as Matt's white-knuckled grip on the saddle horn gradually relaxed. Around them, the other teens had gone quiet, watching intently as Conner showed how to handle an unexpected situation.

"See?" Conner said, patting Dusty's neck. "Sometimes things startle us, but it's how we respond that matters. Right, Rachel?"

Their eyes met across the corral, and Rachel felt the weight of his words. He wasn't just talking about horses.

"That's right," she agreed, moving closer. "The key is staying calm and trusting that you can handle whatever comes your way."

The moment was broken by Tommy Peterson's excited voice. "Mr. Hart, could you tell us about bull riding? Was it scary?"

A shadow crossed Conner's face, but he managed a wry smile. "Scary? Yeah, I'd say so. Bull riding taught me a lot of things—including what happens when you let pride cloud your judgment. But that's a story for another time." He glanced at Rachel. "Right now, let's focus on what Miss Nolan's trying to teach you."

Rachel felt a surge of admiration for how he'd handled the question. The Conner who'd returned to Gold Star Ranch differed from the young man who'd left, and that wasn't a bad thing.

As the morning wore on, she noticed how naturally Conner stepped into a teaching role. He showed the teens how to read their horses' body language, offered quiet encouragement when needed, and shared practical tips drawn from experience.

"You're good with them," she said during a water break, while the teens clustered near the fence, chattering excitedly.

Conner shrugged, but she could see he was pleased. "They remind me of myself at that age. All that energy and uncertainty, trying to figure out where they fit."

"Maybe that's why they respond to you so well." Rachel watched Lisa confidently leading Lightning in a circle, amazed at how far the timid girl had come in just a few hours. "You understand what it's like to be afraid, but choose to be brave, anyway."

Their eyes met. Conner opened his mouth as if to speak, but Tommy's voice interrupted them.

"Miss Nolan! Mr. Hart! Can we try trotting now?"

Rachel smiled at the eager faces turned their way. "What do you think, Mr. Hart? Are they ready?"

Conner's answering grin made her heart skip. "I think they just might be."

The afternoon sun was casting long shadows across the corral when they finally wrapped up the clinic. Rachel's heart swelled with pride as she watched the teens dismount, their faces glowing with accomplishment. Even Lisa, who'd been so terrified at first, was beaming as she patted Lightning's neck.

"Remember to thank your horses," Rachel called out, catching Conner's approving nod. "They've worked hard today, too."

As the teens led their mounts back to the barn, Rachel heard snippets of excited chatter about the upcoming county show. The show had slipped her mind these past few days.

Inside the barn, the usual end-of-lesson bustle filled the air—the clink of hardware being hung up, the soft thuds of saddles being stored, the contented nickering of horses being returned to their stalls. Rachel moved among the activity, offering guidance where needed.

"Mr. Hart?" Lisa approached Conner shyly as he was checking Lightning's hooves. "Thank you for helping me today. I never thought I'd be brave enough to ride again."

Conner straightened, and Rachel saw genuine emotion flash across his face. "You were already brave, Lisa. You just needed someone to remind you of that."

The teen's parents arrived then, and soon the barn was filled with the sounds of goodbyes and thank-yous. Rachel hung back, watching as each teen made a point of saying goodbye to Conner specifically. She noticed how Tommy's father clasped Conner's hand warmly, saying something that made Conner duck his head in that endearingly humble way of his.

Finally, they were alone in the barn. The late afternoon light streamed through the windows, painting everything in warm gold tones. Rachel busied herself with some final tidying, trying to ignore the way her heart quickened when Conner moved to help her.

"That went well," she said, attempting to keep her voice casual. "You're a natural teacher."

"Had a good example to follow," he replied, nodding toward her. Then, after a pause, "Rachel?"

Something in his tone made her look up. Conner stood in a shaft of sunlight, dust motes dancing around him like tiny stars. The vulnerability in his expression made her breath catch.

"About the county show next week..." he began, then seemed to lose his nerve.

Rachel felt a smile tugging at her lips. "Yes?"

"I was wondering..." He rubbed the back of his neck. "Would you consider being my date for it?"

The question hung in the air between them, weighted with more meaning than just a simple invitation. Rachel thought about how far they'd come since his return—the walls that had started to crumble, the trust being rebuilt day by day.

"I'd like that," she said softly.

Conner's answering smile was like a sunrise breaking across his face. "Yeah?"

"Yeah." Rachel felt warmth spread through her chest. "But on one condition."

"Name it."

"Help me get the horses ready for the show. Some of these teens will take part, and I want them to do well."

"Deal," Conner said, without hesitation. Then, with a hint of his old playful smile, "Though I should warn you—I've got a reputation for being particular about show preparations."

Rachel laughed, the sound echoing in the barn. "I remember. You used to drive your father crazy with your attention to detail."

The mention of Warren didn't bring the usual shadow to Conner's eyes. Instead, he looked thoughtful. "Dad always said anything worth doing was worth doing right."

"He did," Rachel agreed. Then, gathering her courage, she added, "You would have made him proud today, you know. Working with those kids, showing them patience and kindness—that's exactly the kind of thing he believed in."

Conner was quiet for a long moment, his eyes fixed on something distant. When he finally spoke, his voice was rough with emotion. "I'm starting to understand why and how he changed so much. Why faith mattered to him." He met her gaze. "Why you mattered to him."

Rachel felt tears prick at the corners of her eyes, but she blinked them away.

"Come on," she said, touching his arm gently. "Let's finish up here. Then maybe we can talk about those show preparations over coffee?"

Conner's smile was answer enough.

Chapter 23

T he golden hour was fading into dusk as Rachel and Conner walked toward the ranch house. The air had cooled, carrying the sweet scent of wild sage and distant pine, and Rachel was acutely aware of Conner's presence beside her. The day's youth clinic had left her pleasantly tired, her heart full from watching those teens discover more of their courage in the saddle.

"Should we sit out here?" he asked, gesturing to the porch swing Warren had installed years ago. The old swing, freshly painted since Conner's return, caught the last rays of sunlight.

Rachel nodded, settling into the familiar seat while Conner went inside. She closed her eyes, letting the events of the day wash over her. The sound of the screen door creaking open made her smile—some things never changed.

"Here you go," Conner said, handing her a cup of coffee before sitting beside her. The swing swayed gently with his weight.

"Thanks."

"Quite a day," Conner said. "Those kids really came alive out there."

Rachel smiled, remembering Lisa's transformation from nervous to triumphant. "You were good with them. Especially Lisa, the way you helped her through her nervousness? That was something special."

"She reminded me of someone," Conner said quietly. "A certain blonde who used to be scared of jumping fences until someone helped her find her nerve."

"I wasn't scared," Rachel protested, though she couldn't help smiling. "I was being cautious."

"Mm hmm." His blue eyes sparkled with amusement. "That's not how I remember it."

The easy banter felt so natural, like slipping into a favorite worn jacket. Rachel took a sip of coffee, feeling the warmth spread through her as the evening coolness touched the air.

"The county show preparations are coming along well, but there's more to do," she said. "Most of the teens from today want to participate."

"About that..." Conner shifted in his chair. "I was thinking I could help more with the preparations. I mean, if you want the help."

Rachel arched an eyebrow. "Even with your notorious perfectionism?"

"Hey now," he chuckled, "Dad always said—"

"'Anything worth doing is worth doing right,'" they finished in unison, and shared a look that held equal parts amusement and nostalgia.

"You handled Tommy's question about bull riding really well today. That couldn't have been easy."

Conner took a long sip of his coffee before responding. "There was a time I couldn't talk about it at all. But today... I don't know. Maybe seeing those kids learning to trust themselves, trust their horses—it reminded me that the past doesn't have to define us."

"No," Rachel agreed softly. "It doesn't."

A comfortable silence settled between them, broken only by the distant nickering of horses and the first cricket songs of the evening. Rachel felt Conner's gaze on her, thoughtful and searching.

"Rachel?" His voice was softer now. "You asked me about my rodeo days when we were out by the river. What about you? What happened with you these past ten years?"

Rachel looked out across the ranch, gathering her thoughts as the sky painted itself in shades of amber and lavender.

"Not really anything different from what I'm doing right now," Rachel finally said, her fingers tracing the rim of her coffee mug. "I worked here on the ranch, continued training horses, got to know your dad better." She paused, a shadow crossing her face. "Lost my father, helped Mom pack up and start her big life adventure."

"Your dad was a good guy?" Conner's voice was gentle. "What happened?"

She nodded, grateful for the simple kindness in his tone. "Heart attack while he was out fixing fences at the house." Her throat tightened at the memory. "Mom... well, she handled it differently than anyone expected."

"How so?"

"She decided life was too short to wait for someday." Rachel smiled softly. "Sold almost everything she owned, gave my sisters and me the house, bought a camper she could pull behind her truck. Now she travels the country, seeing all the places she and Dad talked about visiting 'someday.' She makes stops at ranches that have invited her to train their horses—she's really good at it, you know."

"Like mother, like daughter," Conner said warmly.

Rachel felt his hand move closer to hers. After a moment's hesitation, his fingers gently covered hers. The touch was tentative, as if he was giving her every chance to pull away.

She didn't.

"Does she ever get lonely?" Conner asked. "Out there on her own?"

"I used to worry about that," Rachel admitted. "But she says she feels closest to Dad when she's discovering new places. Says she can almost hear him laughing at her adventures." She turned her hand over beneath his, their fingers naturally intertwining. "Besides, she's made friends all over. Seems like there's always someone inviting her to stay awhile and teach them more about horses."

"Sounds like she found her calling."

"More like she found her freedom," Rachel said thoughtfully. "She taught me something important—that sometimes the bravest thing you can do is open your heart to new possibilities and not get stuck in a life of grief and sadness."

Their eyes met in the deepening twilight. Conner's thumb traced small circles on her palm, sending shivers up her arm.

The first stars were appearing in the darkening sky, pinpricks of light against the deepening indigo. The air had grown cooler, and Rachel shifted slightly closer to Conner's warmth.

"Your dad would be very proud of you, Conner," she said softly. "He always believed in second chances for everyone."

Conner was quiet for a moment, his hand still warm against hers. "I'm starting to understand why and how he changed so much. Why faith mattered to him." He turned to look at her, his blue eyes earnest in the gathering darkness. "Why you mattered to him."

A lone coyote called in the distance, its haunting song echoing across the valley. Rachel thought about Warren Hart, about the man he'd become, about all the conversations they'd shared on this very porch.

"He changed me too, you know," she admitted. "Taught me to never stop believing, never stop hoping, and believe it or not... he taught me forgiveness."

"Tell me more."

She tilted her head slightly, her eyes narrowing, as if trying to read between the words. "What do you mean?"

"Tell me more about you... after I left? I know... I know I hurt you," he said quietly, the weight of his guilt evident in his voice. "I can't imagine the pain I caused. I don't think I've ever stopped regretting it. I was wild, reckless, selfish. You deserved better."

Rachel swallowed hard, her throat tightening at the rawness in his tone, at the memories his words brought back to life. She took a steadying breath, lowering her gaze to where her fingers toyed with the rim of her coffee mug.

How do you put into words the kind of pain that hollowed you out? The kind that took up residence in your chest like a storm and refused to leave? She thought back to the sleepless nights, to days where hope felt like a cruel illusion—haunting, and yet impossible to abandon. How do you explain that even though the man who owned every piece of you walked away without so much as a glance back, you never stopped believing he'd come home? She hadn't just believed it—she had known it deep in her soul, even when she hated herself for it. And maybe that made her foolish. But it also proved what she'd always known to be true: Conner Hart, with all his flaws and rough edges, with all his reckless mistakes, would always be a part of her.

Some people leave, she thought. Conner had left. But the love she'd carried for him never had. It had stayed, stubborn and unyielding, a quiet ember in the darkest corners of her heart.

Letting Conner go had been impossible—not because she couldn't make peace with his mistakes, but because every part of her being told her that his story was entwined with hers. Even through the pain, through the loneliness, through the years, something in her had clung to the idea of him—of who he could be, of who they could be.

She looked back up at him finally, her voice soft but steady. "You broke my heart, Conner. But you never stopped being a part of me."

"When you walked away, it felt like losing a part of myself. And I was so angry at you for that. But..." She paused, gathering the courage to go on. "But even when I was angry, even when it felt like it would never stop hurting, I couldn't stop believing in you. It was like a part of me knew—knew that someday, you'd find your way back."

Her words hung between them, raw and unfaltering, as she met his gaze head-on. "I think I never really let go of you, Conner. Even when I should have."

The silence that followed was thick with emotion, the kind of silence that spoke louder than any words ever could.

"Rachel?"

"Hmm?"

"I've missed this." Conner's voice was rough with emotion. "I've missed you. I never stopped loving you."

The words hung in the air between them, delicate as starlight. Rachel's heart thundered in her chest, equal parts fear and hope warring within her.

"I've missed us too," she said simply, squeezing his hand.

Conner's answering smile was gentle and genuine, full of promises yet to be spoken. Above them, the stars continued their age-old dance across the Montana sky, while somewhere in the distance, the coyote called again to its mate.

On the porch of Gold Star Ranch, two hearts beat in quiet synchronization, finding their way back to a rhythm they'd never quite forgotten.

Chapter 24

Rachel watched Tommy meticulously brush down Star Dancer's coat. They had just finished showcasing the horses at the county show, each one earning impressive winning bids. Yet, as always, Rachel felt a pang of sadness at letting the three horses they had shown go to new homes. It was part of the job, but it never got any easier. The gelding's dark bay coat gleamed under Tommy's careful attention, and Rachel couldn't help but smile at the determination etched on his face.

"Like this, Miss Rachel?" Tommy asked, demonstrating the circular motion she'd taught him.

"Perfect," Rachel nodded, adjusting his grip slightly. "Remember to follow the direction of the hair growth. Star Dancer here appreciates the extra attention."

Beside them, Lisa and Katie worked on settling their horses into their assigned stalls. The girls chatted animatedly about their successful presentations, their excitement infectious.

"Did you see how many people were watching in the stands?" Katie beamed, her blonde ponytail bouncing as she moved. "And Midnight didn't spook once!"

"That's because you've put in the work," Conner's deep voice carried from where he was helping Lisa adjust her horse's water bucket. "Good horsemanship doesn't happen overnight."

Rachel's heart warmed watching him with the teens. He had a natural way with them, firm but encouraging, and they responded to his guidance with eager enthusiasm. It was yet another side of him she was discovering—or rediscovering—since his return. That soft, loving side.

"Mr. Hart?" Lisa looked up from where she was measuring feed. "Will you tell us more about your rodeo days? Tommy says you were famous."

Rachel tensed slightly, but Conner just chuckled, running a hand through his dark hair. "Famous might be stretching it a bit. But I did alright for a while there."

"I would be so scared," Tommy said, pausing in his grooming. "You know, sitting on those bulls?"

"Anyone who says they're not scared of a bull is either lying or crazy," Conner replied honestly. "The trick isn't not being scared—it's using that fear to keep you sharp, to make you respect what you're doing."

Rachel watched him as he spoke, noting how his hand unconsciously went to his shoulder. She could only imagine the scars he must have that lay hidden beneath his shirt. There was something different in how he talked about his rodeo days now—less bravado, more wisdom.

The sound of music drifted across the grounds, and Rachel recognized the opening notes of an old country song. Conner's head lifted, a smile spreading across his face.

"George Strait," he said, then turned to Rachel. "Remember this one?"

Before she could answer, he was crossing the space between them, his blue eyes sparkling. "Let's go dance."

"What?" Rachel blinked, caught off guard by the sudden invitation.

"Come on," he grinned, then turned to the teens. "Y'all got this handled here? These horses are in good hands, right?"

"Yes, sir!" they chorused, exchanging knowing looks that made Rachel's cheeks warm.

"Conner, I—" she started, but he was already taking her hand.

"One dance," he said softly, just for her ears. "For old times' sake."

The warmth of his hand around hers sent familiar tingles up her arm. Rachel nodded, unable to resist the playful light in his eyes or the way her heart leaped at his touch.

"Go on, Miss Rachel!" Katie called after them. "We've got everything under control here!"

"Don't forget to double-check the water buckets!" Rachel called back over her shoulder as Conner led her toward the grandstand area, their joined hands swinging slightly between them.

Rachel was acutely aware of Conner's presence beside her, the way his thumb absently stroked across her knuckles, the familiar scent of his cologne mixed with leather and sunshine.

"I didn't know you still danced," she said, trying to keep her voice light despite the flutter in her stomach.

"Some things you don't forget," he replied, glancing down at her with a smile that made her heart skip. "Like how you always used to step on my toes during the slow songs."

"I did not!" Rachel protested, though she was laughing. "That was one time, at Sadie Miller's wedding, and only because you weren't paying attention to where you were leading me."

"If you say so," he teased, pulling her closer as they reached the dance area.

The grandstand area had been transformed since the livestock show earlier. Strings of lights twinkled overhead, creating a warm glow in the deepening afternoon light. Couples swayed to George Strait's "I Cross My Heart" while others gathered around barrel tables, tapping their boots to the rhythm.

Conner led Rachel to an open spot near the edge of the makeshift dance floor, turning to face her with an easiness that made her breath catch. His hands found their places—one at her waist, the other holding hers—as naturally as if they'd been dancing together all these years.

"See?" he murmured as they began to move. "Some things are just muscle memory."

Rachel tried to focus on the steps, but found herself increasingly aware of how close they were, how his touch seemed to burn through the fabric of her shirt where his hand rested at her waist. The scent of his cologne was intoxicating, bringing back memories of other dances, other moments.

"You're thinking too hard," Conner said softly, giving her hand a gentle squeeze. "Just feel the music."

She looked up at him then, meeting those blue eyes that had always been able to see right through her. "I'm just... surprised, I guess. I didn't think you'd want to dance here, in front of everyone."

His expression softened. "I'm not worried about what everyone thinks. Let them talk. I just want to dance with you."

The simple honesty in his voice made her heart flutter. As they moved together, Rachel gradually relaxed into the rhythm of the music, letting herself enjoy the moment. The music wrapped around them like a comfortable blanket, and she sang along to the lyrics.

"You still know all the words," Conner observed, a smile playing at the corners of his mouth.

"Some things you don't forget," she echoed his earlier words, earning a warm chuckle that she felt rumble through his chest.

As the song drew to a close, neither of them moved to step apart. The band transitioned smoothly into another slow song, and they continued swaying together, lost in their world of shared memories and unspoken possibilities.

The spell was broken by the crackle of the PA system. "Ladies and gentlemen, the bull riding competition will begin in thirty minutes over at the south arena. Competitors, please check in at the chutes."

Rachel felt Conner tense slightly, his rhythm faltering for just a moment before he caught himself. She studied his face, trying to read his expression.

"Do you want to go watch?" she asked carefully, not sure if she wanted him to say yes or no.

To her surprise, he didn't hesitate. "Sure, why not?" His voice was casual, but something flickered in his eyes—something that made Rachel's stomach tighten with worry.

They made their way toward the south arena, their hands still linked. The closer they got, the more the atmosphere changed. The sweet romance of the dance floor gave way to the electric energy of the rodeo crowd. The air filled with the smell of dust and livestock, the sound of bulls snorting in their pens mixing with the excited chatter of spectators.

Rachel felt Conner's grip on her hand tighten as they approached the arena. His eyes scanned the gathering crowd, suddenly his face lit up with recognition.

"Well, I'll be," a voice called out. "If it ain't Conner Hart!"

A tall man with salt-and-pepper hair and weathered features strode toward them, his bow-legged walk marking him as a lifetime cowboy. Rachel recognized him from old rodeo photos and had seen him in Riverbend Valley before—Jake Wheeler, one of Conner's former competitors and friends.

"Jake!" Conner released Rachel's hand to embrace his old friend, slapping him on the back. "Didn't expect to see you here. Thought you were running that training operation down in Texas."

"Still am," Jake grinned, adjusting his black felt cowboy hat. "But I'm here scouting talent, maybe pick up a few promising riders for the circuit." His sharp eyes moved to Rachel. "And this must be the one who got away?"

Rachel felt her cheeks warm as Conner's arm slipped around her waist. "Rachel Nolan," she offered her hand. "Nice to meet you."

"Jake Wheeler. Nice to meet you as well, ma'am. My boy Conner talked about you so much back in the day, feels like I already know you."

They found seats in the bleachers as riders began their warm-ups in the practice pen. Rachel watched Conner's face as his eyes followed each movement, noting how his body seemed to unconsciously shift with the riders' motions. She could almost see him remembering, muscle memory making him lean and adjust as if he were the one in the saddle.

"Miss it?" Jake asked, voicing the question Rachel had been afraid to ask.

Conner was quiet for a moment, his eyes fixed on a young rider adjusting his grip on the rope. "Parts of it," he finally admitted. "The focus, the rush when everything clicks just right. But..." He touched his shoulder absently. "Some prices are too high to pay twice."

Rachel listened. Something in his voice made her study his profile more closely.

"You've got a good eye for talent," Jake continued. "Ever think about judging? Or maybe helping train the next generation? Circuit's always looking for experienced hands to mentor these young guns."

Before Conner could respond, the announcer's voice boomed through the speakers, and the first rider burst from the chute. The crowd roared as the bull spun and bucked; the rider matching each movement with practiced precision.

"See how he's sitting back too far?" Conner leaned close to Rachel's ear to be heard over the noise. "That's gonna cost him if the bull changes direction quick."

Sure enough, seconds later, the bull made a sharp turn, and the rider went flying. Rachel winced, but Conner's commentary continued, pointing out techniques and strategies she'd never noticed before. His voice carried the easy confidence of someone who truly understood his craft, and despite her concerns, she found herself fascinated by this glimpse into his former world.

As rider after rider took their turns, Rachel watched Conner as much as she watched the competition. She saw the way his hands would clench slightly during particularly good rides, how his breath would catch when a rider had a close call. The familiar worry gnawed at her heart—would this always be there, this pull toward the dangerous life he'd left behind?

"Lord," she prayed silently, *"please help me trust that You have a plan for both of us."*

Rachel could almost see the younger Conner, full of dreams and wild ambition. But the man beside her now was different—tempered by time and trials, marked by both failure and grace.

As the last rider finished his run, Jake stood and stretched. "Well, I've got some potential prospects to talk to. Good seeing you, Hart." He paused, then added with a knowing look, "Sometimes the best rides in life aren't the ones on bulls."

After Jake left, Conner turned to Rachel, his eyes serious. "You've been awful quiet."

"Just thinking," she said softly.

"About what?"

"About a lot of different things." She met his gaze steadily.

Conner's hand found hers again, his fingers intertwining with hers. "You know what I was thinking about during all this?"

"What?"

"How grateful I am that my old dreams fell apart." He squeezed her hand. "Because they made room for better ones."

Rachel tilted her head, her heart fluttering as Conner leaned closer. His nearness made her breath catch, the sight of his familiar hazel eyes searching hers, sending a thrill through her. She felt grounded and weightless all at once.

"Rachel, there you are!" Felicia called, her lilting tone snapping her back to reality.

Rachel blinked, turning to see both of her sisters weaving their way through the milling crowd toward them.

"Hey, Rach," Missy greeted warmly, sparing Conner a polite nod. "Afternoon, Conner."

With a quick tip of his hat, Conner replied, "Howdy to you both."

Missy's attention moved back to Rachel, her eyes brimming with excitement. "Want to check out the vendor booths with us?"

Rachel hesitated and glanced up at Conner.

"Go on," he said. "Enjoy some time with your sisters. I'll stick around here and catch up with Jake and a few others for a while."

"Okay," she said, though her heart felt like it was pulling in two directions as she turned to walk away.

Still, she couldn't help but glance back. He was already walking toward the arena floor, blending into the busy crowd.

Chapter 25

Rachel's laughter mingled with her sisters' as they made their way back through the show grounds, their arms laden with small purchases from the vendor booths. The familiar scents of kettle corn and barbecue drifted in the breeze.

"I still can't believe you bought that hideous ceramic rooster," Missy teased, nudging Rachel with her elbow.

"It's not hideous," Rachel protested, adjusting the wrapped package. "It's... unique. Besides, it'll look perfect in the kitchen."

Felicia grinned. "If by perfect you mean perfectly terrifying. Those eyes will haunt your dreams."

"You two are impossible," Rachel laughed, shaking her head.

As they neared the arena, Rachel scanned the crowd for Conner. The stands were empty, but clusters of people still milled about on the arena floor and beyond.

"There he is," Felicia pointed toward the bull pens.

Rachel spotted Conner leaning against one of the steel gates, deep in conversation with Jake. Something in their postures made her pause. The way they were huddled close, leaning in as they spoke. She continued to walk toward them, her sisters following suit.

Jake's voice carried clearly through the air. "...still got the eye for the sport, Conner. Bet it wouldn't take much to climb back on—injuries or not."

Rachel's heart stuttered. She shouldn't eavesdrop, but her feet seemed rooted to the spot as she stood listening to Jake and Conner, their backs facing her.

"It's tempting sometimes, you know?" Conner's response made her blood run cold. "That rush never really leaves you. Maybe I could find a way to be around it again someday—not riding, but coaching, maybe. It's hard to stay away from something that was once your entire world."

"Exactly," Jake agreed enthusiastically. "You've still got a place here in the rodeo world. Lots of folks would see it that way, too."

The ceramic rooster slipped from Rachel's suddenly numb fingers. Felicia caught it before it could shatter on the ground, but the sound of her gasp made both men turn.

"Really, Conner?" The words burst from Rachel's throat, sharp with hurt and anger. "That's your plan now? Jump right back into the life that tore everything apart? The life that nearly got you killed?"

Conner straightened, his face registering shock. "What are you talking about?"

"Forget it." She could feel tears threatening and hated herself for it. "I don't need to hear more. Ride bulls, just go on and do whatever you want—just don't expect me to sit around while you figure out how to break my heart all over again. I knew I should have never trusted you again."

She spun on her heel, nearly colliding with Missy.

"I'll ride home with my sisters," Rachel called over her shoulder, already walking away. Her boots kicked up little clouds of arena dust with each step, matching the storm of emotions churning inside her.

Behind her, she heard Missy's cutting voice, "Good job, cowboy. Didn't take long for you to screw it up, now, did it?"

Rachel quickened her pace, heading for the parking lot. She could hear Felicia's footsteps hurrying to catch up, could practically feel her younger sister's concerned gaze boring into her back.

"Rach, wait," Felicia called softly. "Maybe you should—"

"Don't." Rachel's voice cracked. "Please, just... don't."

They reached Missy's truck just as their younger sister caught up with them. Rachel climbed into the back seat, grateful when neither sister tried to make her talk. As Missy started the engine, Rachel leaned her forehead against the cool window glass.

"I can't believe him," Rachel said, her voice low but trembling with disappointment. "I really thought I could trust him this time."

Felicia turned to look at her sister, her tone gentle yet measured. "Rachel, we didn't hear everything. For all we know, they were just talking. Don't let your mind run away before you understand the entire story."

Missy turned to face Rachel as well, her expression a mix of concern and quiet frustration. "Felicia might be right, but honestly, Rachel has every right to feel the way she does."

Rachel tried to swallow the lump rising in her throat, but her voice broke as she finally said, "What would either of you have thought if you were in my position?"

***

Conner watched helplessly as Rachel disappeared into the crowd, her sisters flanking her like protective shadows. The ceramic rooster Felicia had caught sat abandoned on a nearby barrel, its painted eyes seeming to mock him.

"Well, son," Jake sighed, adjusting his hat. "You sure stepped in it this time. But what is it you stepped in has got me?"

"I have an idea. I wasn't even saying I'm going back to the rodeo." Conner ran a frustrated hand through his hair. "I was just talking, thinking out loud about maybe teaching someday—"

"Well, she might not have heard our whole conversation. Or, sometimes folks hear only what they want to." Jake's weathered face softened with understanding. "But that girl? She cares plenty about you, Conner. I wouldn't let this go. You need to set things straight."

Conner's jaw clenched as he stared in the direction Rachel had gone. "She doesn't trust me..."

"Can you blame her?" Jake asked quietly. "Way I remember it, you lit out of here like your tail was on fire, never looked back once."

"That was ten years ago," Conner protested, but the words felt hollow, even to his own ears.

"Some hurts don't care how long ago they happened." Jake pushed away from the gate. "Question is, what are you gonna do about it now?"

Conner touched his shoulder absently, feeling the familiar pull of scar tissue beneath his shirt. "I don't know."

A low rumble of thunder rolled across the fairgrounds, matching Conner's darkening mood. Around them, people hurried to pack up before the approaching storm hit, but Conner barely noticed.

Jake clapped him on the shoulder. "Well, I've got a couple more prospects to talk to before this weather hits. But Conner?" He waited until the younger man met his eyes. "Sometimes the biggest rides in life ain't the ones on bulls. They're the ones where you gotta hold on tight to what matters most."

Chapter 26

Conner gripped the steering wheel of the ranch truck as he turned onto the gravel driveway leading to the Nolan family home. The empty horse trailer rattled behind him, its hollow sounds matching the emptiness in his chest. Rachel's truck was noticeably absent, but both Missy's truck and Felicia's sedan sat in the circular drive.

Thunder rumbled in the distance as Conner pulled to a stop, the air heavy with the promise of rain. He sat for a moment, gathering his thoughts. The outdoor lights cast shadows across the front porch, highlighting the familiar rocking chairs where he'd spent countless evenings with Rachel in their younger days.

The screen door's hinges creaked as Felicia stepped out onto the porch before Conner could even climb the steps. Her expression was guarded, but not unkind, as she watched him approach.

"She's not here," Felicia said softly, answering his unspoken question.

Conner stopped at the bottom of the stairs. "I need to talk to her, Felicia. Help me understand what happened back at the show. What upset her so much?"

Felicia studied him for a long moment, then gestured to one of the rocking chairs. "Maybe you should sit down."

Conner climbed the steps, the old wood groaning beneath his weight. He settled into the rocking chair, while Felicia leaned against the porch railing, her arms crossed loosely. A wind chime tinkled softly in the growing breeze, its gentle music a stark contrast to the tension in the air.

"Rachel heard you talking with Jake about getting back into the rodeo world," Felicia began carefully.

"But I wasn't—" Conner started to protest, but Felicia held up a hand.

"Let me finish. She heard you talking about coaching, about being around that life again." Felicia's voice softened. "To you, it might have just been a conversation, maybe even just thinking out loud. But to Rachel? It sounded like history repeating itself."

Conner leaned forward, running a hand through his hair in frustration. "I wasn't planning to leave. I was just talking about maybe teaching someday, maybe starting a program on the ranch, helping young riders—"

"Men just don't get it sometimes," Missy's voice cut through the evening air as she stepped out onto the porch, the screen door banging shut behind her. She carried three glasses of sweet tea, passing them around before settling into a rocking chair. "Rachel doesn't hear 'maybe someday.' She hears 'I'm leaving again.'"

"I wouldn't—" Conner began.

"You already did once before," Missy pointed out, though her usual sharp edge was tempered with something almost like sympathy. "Ten years ago, you packed up and disappeared without a word. Left her standing there with nothing but broken promises and a whole lot of questions."

Thunder rolled closer, and the first few drops of rain began to fall, pattering against the porch roof. Conner gripped his glass of tea, condensation cool against his palms.

"I was young and stupid back then," he said quietly. "I've changed."

"Have you?" Felicia asked gently. "Because from where Rachel was standing today, it looked an awful lot like you were getting pulled back into that world. The same world that took you away from her before."

"It's not that simple," Conner protested, setting his untouched tea on the small table between the chairs. "The rodeo circuit isn't my life anymore. I learned that lesson the hard way."

"But it shaped who you are," Felicia pointed out. "And Rachel... she's spent years building defenses to protect herself from that kind of hurt again, whether or not she wants to admit it."

Missy shifted in her chair, the wood creaking beneath her. "You know what the worst part was way back then?" Her voice had lost its usual edge, replaced by a quiet sadness. "She blamed herself for everything. Convinced herself she wasn't enough."

The words hit Conner like a bull had rammed his chest. Rain was falling steadily now, creating a curtain of water beyond the porch's shelter. Lightning flickered in the distance, illuminating the pain on his face.

"I never meant—" he swallowed hard. "She has to know that wasn't true."

"Does she?" Felicia asked. "Because all she knows is that one day you were here, planning a future together, and the next day you were gone. No explanation, no goodbye. Just... gone."

"And now," Missy added, "she hears you talking about getting involved in that world again, even if it's just teaching. Can you blame her for being scared?"

Conner leaned back in the chair, his chest tight with guilt and frustration. "I came back to build a new life, make things right. To rebuild what I broke."

"That's just it, Conner," Felicia said softly. "You can't rebuild something overnight. Trust isn't earned with grand gestures or pretty words. It's built day by day, choice by choice."

Lightning flashed again, closer this time, followed almost immediately by a crack of thunder that shook the porch windows. Conner stood, pacing the length of the porch as he struggled to find the right words.

"I know I messed up," he finally said, stopping to face Rachel's sisters. "Back then, I was so caught up in my dreams, my pride, that I couldn't see what I was throwing away. I was so angry with my dad back then. But being with Rachel now..." He trailed off, emotion thick in his voice.

"Makes you want to fix everything right away," Missy finished for him. "But Rachel's not some spooked horse you can gentle with a few kind words and treats."

"She's right," Felicia added. "Rachel needs to see that you're not just here until something better comes along. That she's not your backup plan?"

Conner turned to face them fully, his expression fierce. "She was never my backup plan. Even when I was being an idiot chasing rodeo glory, she was always..." He stopped, running a hand over his face. "She deserves better than what I gave her."

"Well," Missy said, "at least you're not completely dense."

"What do I do?" Conner asked, the question hanging in the rain-heavy air. "How do I prove to her that this time is different?"

Felicia exchanged a look with Missy before answering. "You show her through actions, not words. Every single day, you choose her. You choose this life, this place, this future. Not because you have to, but because you want to."

"And you don't run," Missy added firmly. "When things get hard, when the rodeo memories come calling, when the old life tempts you—you plant your feet and you stay. Because that's what Rachel needs to see."

Thunder rolled overhead as Conner absorbed their words. The rain had intensified, drumming against the roof in a steady rhythm that matched the pounding of his heart.

"You know," Felicia said thoughtfully, "Rachel was there when your daddy found his faith. She saw how a person can truly change when they let God guide their path." She paused, studying Conner's face. "She's seen real transformation before. Maybe that's why she's so scared now—because she wants to believe you've changed, but the cost of being wrong is too high."

Conner leaned against one of the porch posts, his voice rough with emotion. "I have changed. Not just because I want her back, but because I finally understand what matters. What genuine love looks like."

"Then prove it," Missy challenged, her tone softer than before. "Not with grand gestures or promises. Prove it by being there. By showing up every day. By choosing her and this life, even when it's hard. Choosing her, over and over and over."

Lightning split the sky again, illuminating the determination on Conner's face. "I will," he said firmly. "Whatever it takes, however long it takes. I'm not the same man who left ten years ago."

"No," Felicia agreed quietly. "You're not. But Rachel needs time to see that for herself, repeatedly."

Conner straightened, his decision clear in his stance. "I'm not giving up." He glanced at the empty driveway where Rachel's truck should have been. "Any idea where she might have gone?"

Missy and Felicia exchanged another look, this one heavy with meaning. "She probably went to one of the places she always goes when she needs to think," Missy said carefully.

"The creek behind the ranch," Conner said immediately, remembering the quiet spot where they'd spent so many evenings in their youth. "By the old oak tree."

"Conner," Felicia called as he started down the porch steps, "be careful with her heart. She's stronger than she was ten years ago, but that just means she's got more to lose."

He paused in the rain, turning back to face them. "I know. And I promise you both—I'm going to earn her trust back, one day at a time."

"Well," Missy said, a reluctant smile tugging at her lips, "maybe you're not completely hopeless after all."

Thunder rumbled overhead as Conner strode through the downpour to the truck. Behind him, the sisters watched from the porch, their expressions a mix of hope and concern.

"You think he'll get it right this time?" Missy asked softly.

Felicia wrapped an arm around her sister's shoulders. "I think he's finally ready to try. The rest is up to Rachel... and God's timing."

As Conner pulled away, wipers fighting the heavy rain, he sent up a silent prayer. "Lord, help me find the right words. Help me show her that this time is different. That I'm different."

The storm raged on as he drove toward the ranch, toward Rachel, toward what he hoped would be a chance to prove that sometimes love deserves a second ride—if you're brave enough to hold on.

Chapter 27

The rain fell in heavy sheets as Conner navigated the familiar dirt road. Lightning illuminated the countryside in stark flashes, each burst revealing the muddy path ahead. He knew the way to the creek by heart—could probably walk it blindfolded—but tonight, every mile felt weighted with consequence.

The truck's headlights caught the old fence line, and Conner's grip tightened on the steering wheel. Beyond those ancient posts and the tangle of oak trees lay the creek where he and Rachel had shared so many quiet moments. Where she'd first told him she loved him. Where he'd made promises he'd failed to keep.

Thunder cracked overhead as he spotted Rachel's truck parked in the shadows near the trailhead. Relief and apprehension warred in his chest—she was here, probably soaked to the bone in this weather, but here. Conner killed the engine, and for a moment, just sat listening to the drumming of rain against the roof, gathering his courage.

The storm had intensified, transforming the usually serene path into a treacherous maze of mud and shadows. But Conner barely noticed the rain soaking through his shirt as he made his way down the trail, guided more by memory than sight. Each step brought him closer to Rachel, and to the moment of truth they both needed to face.

Lightning flashed again, illuminating the massive oak tree ahead. Through the curtain of rain, Conner spotted Rachel's figure beneath its sprawling branches. She stood with her back to him, one hand pressed against the rough bark, her clothes soaked through. Even from this distance, he could see the tension in her shoulders.

"Rachel," he called, his voice nearly lost in the storm.

She stiffened, but didn't turn around. "Go away, Conner."

Instead, he stepped closer, closing the distance between them. The old oak tree's canopy provided little shelter from the rain, but neither of them seemed to notice the weather anymore. Water dripped from Rachel's honey-blonde hair, now darkened to amber by the rain.

"I can't do that," he said. "Not this time."

Rachel whirled to face him, her hazel eyes bright with tears. "Why not? You were so good at it before."

The words struck him like physical blows, but he held his ground. "I deserve that. I deserve every bit of anger you've got stored up. And I want you to let it out. Let me have it. But I need you to hear me out as well."

"Hear you out?" She laughed, but the sound held no joy. "I heard plenty at the show, Conner. About how you're thinking of getting back into the rodeo world. How you miss it. How—"

"That's not completely what I was saying," he cut in, taking another step closer. "If you'd heard the whole conversation—"

"Why?" Rachel's voice cracked. "So I could hear you planning your escape all over again? Listen to you talk about how much you miss that life?" She wrapped her arms around herself, as if trying to hold herself together. "I can't do it, Conner. I won't."

Thunder rolled overhead as Conner fought the urge to reach for her. "Rachel, please. I'm not planning to leave. I'm not plotting some escape. What you heard—"

"What I heard," she cut him off, "was you talking about getting back into that world. The same world that took you away before. The same life that just about killed you." Her voice broke on the last words, revealing the fear beneath her anger.

Conner stepped closer, the rain streaming down his face. "I was talking about maybe teaching someday. Here, at the ranch. About using what I learned—even my mistakes—to help keep other riders safe." He swallowed hard. "But that's not even what this is really about, is it?"

Rachel turned away, but not before he caught the flash of pain in her eyes. "Don't."

"I'm not leaving, ever again," he pressed on, his voice gentle but firm.

"Aren't you?" She spun back to face him, and this time he couldn't tell if it was rain or tears on her cheeks. "It's what you do, Conner. When things get hard, when life gets too real, you run. You always have."

"Not anymore." He took another step closer, close enough now to see the way she trembled. "I'm not that same stupid kid who thought glory was more important than love and family. Who was too blind to see what really mattered."

"Pretty words," Rachel whispered, but he could hear the longing beneath her skepticism. "You were always good with those."

"You want more than words?" Conner's voice roughened with emotion. "Look around you, Rachel. Look at where we are." He gestured to the oak tree looming above them. "Right here, under this tree, is where you first told me you loved me. Where I promised you forever." He paused, pain etching his features.

Rachel's breath caught audibly. "Why are you doing this?"

"Because I need you to understand something." Lightning flashed, illuminating the intensity of his blue eyes. "Every morning when I wake up at the ranch, every time I see you, every moment I spend trying to rebuild what I broke—it's not because of some obligation. It's because this is where I want to be. Where I choose to be."

The rain continued to fall, but Rachel seemed frozen in place, her hazel eyes locked on his face as if searching for any sign of deception.

"I've changed, Rachel," he continued softly. "Not just because of my injuries, not just because I want you back. But because I finally understand what matters. What genuine love looks like."

"And what's that?" Her voice was barely a whisper.

"It's showing up. Every day. It's choosing the same person over and over again, even when it's hard. Even when you're scared." He took another step closer. "It's what you did for my father when he was struggling. What you do for every broken horse that comes to the ranch. What I should have done for you ten years ago."

Rachel's composure cracked slightly. "Conner—"

"I know you're scared," he pressed on. "You have every right to be. But I'm not asking you to trust me right away. I'm asking for a chance to earn that trust back, day by day, choice by choice."

Rachel took a shuddering breath, raindrops clinging to her eyelashes. "How can I?" she asked, her voice catching. "How can I trust that the next time someone mentions the rodeo circuit, or the next time an opportunity comes along, you won't—"

"Because now I understand what I'd be losing," Conner interrupted, his voice raw with emotion. "Because I've lived with regret for ten years. Because every morning when I wake up and see this ranch, see you—" He stopped, struggling to find the right words. "Rachel, leaving you was the biggest mistake of my life. I won't make it twice."

Another crack of thunder shook the air around them. Rachel wrapped her arms tighter around herself, but Conner noticed she didn't step away when he moved closer.

"You know what I see when I look at you?" he asked softly. "I see someone who never gave up on believing in me. Someone who can take something broken and help it heal. Someone who's stronger than I ever was. I see love when I look at you. I see a life and a future that I want."

"Stop," Rachel whispered, but there was less fight in her voice now.

"No," Conner said firmly. "Because you need to hear this. I'm not here because of your sisters' lectures, or because of my father's will, or because I need somewhere to land safely. I'm here because this is where I belong. Where I always belonged."

Lightning flashed again, and in that brief, brilliant moment, their eyes met. The years seemed to fall away, leaving only the raw, honest truth between them.

"I'm terrified," Rachel admitted, her voice barely audible above the rain. "Not just of you leaving again, but of how much I still—" She cut herself off, looking away.

"How much you still what?" Conner asked gently, taking another step closer. They were barely a foot apart now, the rain creating a private world around them.

"How much I still feel for you," Rachel whispered, finally meeting his gaze. "Even after everything. Even when I tell myself, I shouldn't." A sob caught in her throat. "I can't go through losing you again, Conner. I won't survive it."

Without thinking, Conner reached out, his hand cupping her cheek. To his surprise, she didn't pull away. "You will not lose me," he said firmly. "I know words aren't enough. I know I have to prove it. And I will—every single day, for as long as it takes."

Rachel leaned into his touch almost unconsciously, tears mixing with the rain on her face. "I want to believe you," she breathed.

"Then believe," he said softly.

Another flash of lightning illuminated them, standing so close beneath the old oak tree where their story had begun. Where, perhaps, it could begin again.

"I'm still angry at you," Rachel warned, but her voice held a note of something else now—hope, maybe, or the beginning of forgiveness.

"You have every right to be," Conner acknowledged. "I'm not asking you to forget what happened. I'm just asking for a chance to prove that this time is different. That I'm different."

Rachel studied his face for a long moment, searching. Then, slowly, she nodded. "Day by day," she said quietly.

"Day by day," Conner agreed, his heart swelling with cautious hope.

They stood there in the rain, neither moving closer nor pulling away. It wasn't forgiveness—not yet. But it was a beginning.

Above them, the storm began to ease; the thunder growing more distant. Through a break in the clouds, a single star peeked through, its light reflecting on the raindrops still falling around them.

"Sometimes," Conner thought, *"love deserves a second ride. Not because it's easy, but because it's worth fighting for. Worth staying for. Worth proving, day by day, choice by choice, that some things—some people—are meant to be part of your forever."*

Chapter 28

The next morning dawned clear and bright, washing away the last traces of the storm. But evidence of the night's rainfall remained—puddles dotting the ranch yard, mud squelching under boots, and a tangible freshness in the air that spoke of new beginnings.

Rachel moved through her morning routine at the stables, her mind replaying the previous night's conversation with Conner beneath the old oak tree. Every time she closed her eyes, she could see him standing there in the rain, making promises she wanted desperately to believe. But it was what he did today—and every day after—that would truly matter.

Her hands stilled on the curry brush as she heard footsteps approaching the barn. Taking a deep breath, she turned to face whatever this new day would bring.

The sound of boots on gravel drew closer. Her heart quickened its pace.

"Morning," Conner's voice was quiet, careful. He stood in the doorway, holding two travel mugs of coffee.

She accepted one of the mugs with a small nod. "Morning." Their fingers brushed during the exchange, and she tried to ignore the warmth that sparked at the contact.

She wrapped her hands around the warm cup, thankful for the distraction it provided, as part of her wanted to reach for Conner's hand and apologize for her emotional outburst yesterday. Yet another part of her knew her reasons for reacting that way were valid.

"I was thinking," Conner said, setting his coffee down on a nearby shelf. "Maybe we could work with one of the mares today. The one dad bought just before..." He trailed off, but Rachel understood.

"Spirit," she supplied, referring to the skittish palomino that had Warren had bought at the beginning of the year. "She's been difficult. Doesn't trust easily." The parallel wasn't lost on either of them.

Conner's lips curved slightly. "Then maybe we can show her that sometimes trust is worth the risk."

Rachel took another sip of coffee, using the moment to study him. He looked tired, like he had slept little, but there was something different in his bearing—a steadiness.

"Alright," she agreed. "But Conner?" She waited until his blue eyes met hers. "Day by day, remember? Don't push me."

His expression softened with understanding. "Day by day," he echoed. "That's all I'm asking for."

The morning sun climbed higher as they made their way to Spirit's paddock. The palomino mare watched their approach warily, her golden coat gleaming in the light, ears pricked forward with nervous attention.

"She sure is a beauty," Conner breathed, taking in the horse's proud carriage and delicate features.

"And wild at times," Rachel added, unlatching the gate carefully. "Your dad bought her from a rescue situation. The previous owner used heavy hands and harsh methods." She glanced at Conner. "Sometimes the deepest wounds are the ones you can't see."

Conner absorbed her words, understanding the double meaning.

"We need patience," Rachel replied, moving slowly into the paddock. "Consistency." She stopped and glanced over her shoulder at Conner before continuing to speak. "You prove yourself trustworthy through actions, not words." She reached into her pocket, producing a few sugar cubes. "And sometimes, you offer something sweet to show your intentions."

Spirit snorted, taking a few tentative steps closer, drawn by Rachel's gentle presence and the promise of treats. Rachel remained still, letting the mare make her own choice.

Conner observed quietly.

"They're honest creatures. They don't play games or make promises they can't keep. They just... are."

"Unlike people," Conner said.

"Unlike people," she agreed, watching as Spirit finally stepped close enough to delicately take a sugar cube from her palm.

The morning continued in a dance of careful movements and quiet communication, both with Spirit and each other. Rachel demonstrated her gentle approach, showing Conner how to earn the mare's trust through patience and consistent kindness.

"See how she's licking and chewing?" Rachel pointed out as Spirit processed their latest interaction. "That's her way of saying she's thinking about trusting us."

Conner nodded, keeping his voice low and steady. "Like she's weighing the risk against the reward."

"Exactly." Rachel handed him a lead rope. "Your turn. Remember—slow and steady."

As Conner stepped forward, Rachel watched him approach the mare. His movements differed from the brash young man he used to be, more measured, more thoughtful now. Spirit's ears swiveled toward him, but she didn't retreat.

"That's it," Rachel encouraged softly. "Let her come to you."

Conner stood quietly, rope loose in his hands, waiting. After what seemed like an eternity, Spirit stretched her neck forward, nostrils flaring as she caught his scent.

"She's reading your intention," Rachel explained. "Horses can sense when someone's being genuine."

"Like people?" Conner asked, his eyes meeting hers over Spirit's back.

Rachel felt her breath catch at the intensity in his gaze. "Sometimes better than people," she managed.

The moment was broken by the sound of a truck pulling into the ranch yard. Rachel recognized Jake in the passenger seat.

"Looks like your buddy's here," she said.

"It can wait," Conner said, still focused on Spirit. "This is more important."

The simple statement, delivered without fanfare or expectation, touched something in Rachel's heart. One small choice, one moment of choosing what mattered most.

Rachel watched as Conner maintained his patient stance with Spirit, even as Jake's footsteps approached the paddock. The mare's ears flicked back at the new sound, but she remained near Conner, a small victory that brought a smile to his face.

"Well, look at this," Jake's voice carried across the morning air. "Never thought I'd see Conner Hart playing horse whisperer."

"Learning from the best," Conner replied softly, his eyes still on Spirit as he carefully clipped the lead rope to her halter. The mare accepted the connection without protest, drawing another smile from Rachel.

Jake leaned against the fence, watching them work. "Sorry to interrupt, but we need to discuss those breeding contracts before the Wilsons arrive next week."

Conner gave Spirit a final pat before turning to Jake. "Can we meet later this afternoon instead? I promised to help with Spirit's training this morning."

Rachel felt something warm unfurl in her chest at his words. It wasn't just that he'd chosen to stay—it was the natural way he'd done it, without hesitation or show.

"Sure thing," Jake agreed easily, pushing off the fence. "Just don't forget, those contracts need reviewing." He tipped his hat to Rachel before heading back to his truck.

When they were alone again, Rachel studied Conner's profile. "You didn't have to do that," she said. "The contracts are important."

"So is this," he replied simply, running a gentle hand down Spirit's neck. "You know, I meant what I said about learning from the best." He glanced at her, a hint of his old charm showing through. "Even if the teacher is tough."

Rachel felt a smile tugging at her lips despite herself. "Tough, huh?"

"The toughest," Conner confirmed, but his smile was warm. "And the best."

They worked together for the rest of the morning, guiding Spirit through basic groundwork exercises. The mare grew more confident with each successful interaction, though she still startled occasionally at sudden movements.

"She's like a mirror," Rachel observed as they took a water break around noon. "Every reaction reflects something about her past experiences."

Conner leaned against the fence post, considering her words. "How do you help her move past those experiences?"

"You show her that the past doesn't have to define her future," Rachel said quietly, aware they weren't just talking about the horse anymore. "You prove new experiences can differ from old ones."

The sun had reached its peak, casting brief shadows across the paddock. Spirit grazed peacefully nearby, more relaxed than Rachel had seen her since her arrival at the ranch.

"Thank you," Conner said suddenly, his voice serious.

Rachel turned to look at him. "For what?"

"For giving me a chance to learn." He met her gaze steadily. "Not just about the horses, but about doing things right. About being patient. About earning trust instead of expecting it."

Rachel felt her heart flutter, but kept her voice steady. "Day by day, remember?"

"Day by day," he agreed, then added softly, "But some days are better than others."

Looking at Spirit's progress, at the peaceful morning they'd shared, Rachel had to agree. Some days were definitely better than others.

As they led Spirit back to her stall, the mare following with new-found trust, Rachel couldn't help but notice how naturally she and Conner had fallen back into working together. Their movements had fallen into a peaceful rhythm, anticipating each other's needs without words—just like in the old days.

"She did well today," Conner said, as they secured the stall door. "Better than I expected."

"Sometimes that's all it takes," Rachel replied, gathering up their equipment. "One good day to show that change is possible."

Conner helped her put away the leads and brushes, their hands brushing occasionally in the familiar dance of barn chores. "I should probably go find Jake," he said finally, though he made no move to leave. "Get those contracts sorted out instead of putting it off."

Rachel nodded, fighting the unexpected disappointment that rose at the thought of him leaving. "Probably should."

"But first—" He hesitated, then pressed on. "Would you join me for dinner tonight? Nothing fancy, just at the house."

Rachel felt her pulse quicken. "Just dinner?" she asked carefully.

"Just dinner," he confirmed. "And conversation. Whatever you're comfortable with." His blue eyes held hers steadily. "No pressure, no expectations. Just... another day."

Rachel nodded before she could overthink it. "Okay. Dinner."

The smile that lit up his face reminded her of younger days, but there was something different in it now—something more mature, more genuine. "Six o'clock?"

"Six o'clock," she agreed.

As Conner headed toward the main house, Rachel stayed in the barn. Spirit nickered softly from her stall, drawing Rachel's attention.

"I know, girl," she whispered, reaching out to stroke the mare's nose. "Trust is a risk. But maybe..." She glanced toward where Conner had disappeared, remembering his steady presence throughout the morning, his quiet choices, his patience. "Maybe some risks are worth taking. Day by day."

The mare pressed her velvet nose into Rachel's palm, as if agreeing. Through the barn doors, Rachel could see the sun shining on puddles from last night's storm, their surfaces smooth and clear in the afternoon light. Like everything else, storms passed, leaving the world fresh and new—if you were brave enough to step into the aftermath and see what might grow.

Chapter 29

Rachel stood before her bedroom mirror, running a brush through her hair for the third time. "It's just dinner," she reminded her reflection firmly. But the flutter in her stomach suggested otherwise.

She'd changed outfits twice already, finally settling on a soft blue sundress that she hadn't worn in ages. Not too dressy for a casual dinner, but nicer than her usual ranch wear. Her sisters' voices echoed in her head, teasing her about fussing over her appearance, but she pushed the thoughts aside.

The clock on her bedside table read 5:40. Time to go, unless she wanted to be late. Late, or chicken out entirely, which was starting to feel tempting. Rachel grabbed her keys, then hesitated, remembering the night before in the rain. Day by day, they'd agreed. And today... today was just another day.

But as she headed down the stairs, she couldn't quite convince her racing heart of that.

The drive to Conner's house seemed both too long and too short. Rachel parked beside Conner's truck, noticing the porch lights were already on, casting a soft glow out into the gathering dusk.

She checked her reflection one last time in the rearview mirror, tucking a strand of hair behind her ear. "Just dinner," she whispered to herself, but her fingers still trembled slightly as she reached for the door handle.

Before she could knock, the front door opened. Conner stood there, dressed in clean jeans and a blue button-down shirt that brought out the color of his eyes. His hair was still damp from a recent shower, and Rachel caught the scent of his soap—a mix of pine, musk, and something uniquely him she remembered all too well.

"You look beautiful," he said.

Rachel stepped past him into the house, noticing changes since he had made. The living room had been tidied, a lot of Warren's clutter was now gone, fresh flowers sat in a vase on the coffee table, and something delicious simmered in the kitchen.

"I hope you're hungry," Conner said, following her inside. "I might have gone a little overboard."

"You cooked?" Rachel couldn't keep the surprise from her voice.

A faint blush colored his cheeks. "Don't sound so shocked. I've learned a few things over the years." He paused, then added, "Had to, after I left. Couldn't live on takeout forever."

The casual mention of his time away hung between them for a moment, but somehow it felt less painful than before. Perhaps because he'd said it without defensiveness or guilt.

"Something smells amazing," Rachel said, following Conner into the kitchen, which opened into the dining room. She stopped short at the sight before her. The old oak table had been set with care—Warren's good dishes, she noticed, and a pair of candles waiting to be lit. A bottle of wine breathed nearby.

"Just casual, huh?" she teased gently, trying to mask how touched she was by the effort.

Conner rubbed the back of his neck. "Maybe I got a little carried away. We can eat on the porch if this is too—"

"It's perfect," Rachel interrupted softly. "Just... unexpected."

He moved to the stove, lifting the lid on a pot that filled the kitchen with the aroma of herbs and garlic. "I made Dad's old recipe for beef burgundy. At least, I tried to. Never could get it quite like his."

Rachel's heart squeezed at the mention of Warren. "He used to make this for special occasions."

"And many Sunday dinners," Conner added, stirring the pot gently. "Remember how he'd spend all day cooking, pretending he wasn't checking the pot every five minutes?"

A smile tugged at Rachel's lips. "And how he'd act all casual about it, but you could tell how proud he was when we asked for seconds."

Their eyes met over the steaming pot, sharing a moment of bittersweet remembrance. In the soft kitchen light, Rachel could see the shadows of grief still lingering on Conner's face.

"Have you ever wondered what might have happened if I'd stayed and not left all those years ago?"

Rachel leaned against the counter. "Yes."

Conner gazed out the window at the distant pasture. "I've been thinking about that a lot lately. Last night, something really profound hit me. I was sitting alone on the porch in the darkness, couldn't sleep. It was well after midnight."

He turned toward Rachel, studying her. The most beautiful woman he had ever laid eyes on. The woman who held his heart in her palm and never gave up on him.

"I honestly believe my leaving was what made Dad quit drinking. It took losing me for him to realize how fragile life is. After he lost everything that mattered most, he hit rock bottom. And Rachel..."

"Yes?"

"I walked the same path," Connor said, his voice catching. "Had to lose everything to find what truly matters."

Rachel's gentle nod spoke volumes of understanding.

"Like father, like son," she murmured softly.

"The irony is crushing sometimes." His voice trembled. "Dad and I, we left so much devastation in our wake, Rachel. Both had to hit rock bottom alone before we could see the beauty of God's plan. And you..." He turned to face her fully. "You never gave up on either of us. Your faith in God's ability to restore what was broken... it humbles me."

Their eyes met, years of unspoken feelings flowing between them. As Connor lit the candles on the table, their warm glow illuminated tears that neither tried to hide.

"Would you like some wine?" he asked, gesturing to the bottle.

Rachel nodded, accepting the glass he poured.

Conner's hand trembled slightly as he served the beef burgundy onto Warren's old plates. Rachel observed quietly, taking her seat at the table.

Conner settled into his own chair. The candlelight flickered between them, casting warm shadows across the dining room.

Rachel took a small bite of the beef burgundy, pleasantly surprised by the rich flavor. "This is good," she said honestly. "Different from Warren's, but good in its own way."

Conner relaxed slightly at her approval. "I tried to get it right, just like dad used to make it."

They ate in comfortable silence for a moment, the only sounds the gentle clink of silverware and the distant chorus of crickets through the open window.

"You were amazing with Spirit today. The way you handled her, how you knew exactly what she needed..."

Rachel smiled, grateful for the shift to safer ground. "She's a special horse. Reminds me a bit of that paint mare we had years ago. Do you remember Star?

"How could I forget?" Conner chuckled. "She was the first horse that ever threw me."

"And the one that I was training before..." Rachel trailed off, the memory catching in her throat.

Conner set down his fork, his expression serious. "Before I left." He didn't shy away from it this time. "Rachel, there's something I need to say about that."

She tensed slightly, but nodded for him to continue.

"I've spent ten years regretting how I left, what I threw away. But today, watching you with Spirit, I realized something." He paused, choosing his words carefully. "I was like that mare back then, wild, untamed, thinking freedom meant running away from everything that mattered."

"Conner—"

"Please, let me finish," he said gently. "I needed to grow up, to learn some hard lessons. I needed to get away from my dad... and I know that sounds awful, but it's the truth. But I never stopped loving you. Even when I was too stubborn to admit it, too proud to come back to you, too scared to face what I'd done. That love was always there."

Rachel's hands trembled around her wineglass. "Why are you telling me this now?

"Because you deserve to know the truth. All of it." His voice was steady, though his eyes betrayed his emotion. "And because I want you to understand that while I can't change the past, I know exactly what I want for my future."

Rachel's heart thundered in her chest as she met his gaze across the candlelit table. "And what is it you want?" she asked softly, though part of her feared the answer.

"This," Conner gestured to encompass the room, the ranch, everything. "Home. The life my father built. The chance to make things right." He paused, his voice dropping lower. "You."

Rachel set down her wineglass carefully. "Conner—"

"I know it's not that simple," he continued quickly. "I know I have to earn back your trust, prove that I've changed. And I will. But I need you to know that I'm not confused about what I want. I'm not that restless kid looking for the next big thrill. I'm not that kid that runs from problems at home instead of staying and facing them head on."

"How can you be certain?" The question slipped out before Rachel could stop it. "How do you know you won't wake up one morning and just decide to leave?"

Conner leaned forward, his expression earnest in the flickering candlelight. "Because I've lived that other life. I've chased every thrill, followed every road out there. And you know what I learned?" He waited until she met his eyes. "None of it meant anything without someone to share it with. Without love."

Rachel felt tears threatening and blinked them back. "Love isn't always enough."

"No," he agreed softly. "It takes commitment. Choice. Faith." He reached across the table, his hand stopping just short of hers. "That's what my father finally understood, isn't it? What you helped him see?"

Rachel nodded, unable to speak past the lump in her throat.

"Then help me understand too," he whispered.

Rachel stared at Conner's hand, resting just inches from hers on the white tablecloth. The candlelight caught the small scars on his knuckles—evidence of years of hard work and harder falls.

"There are some things you have to figure out on your own. I can't do all the heavy lifting," she said finally, her voice gentle but firm.

"You're right. But maybe... maybe we could figure it out together? Day by day?"

The phrase they'd been sharing hung in the air between them, weighted with new meaning. Rachel felt something shift in her heart, like a key turning in a long-rusted lock.

"I choose you. Today, tomorrow, and all the days after. However long it takes Rachel."

Chapter 30

Sunlight streamed through Rachel's bedroom window as she fastened the last pearl button on her lavender dress.

"Rachel! Have you seen my white cardigan?" Missy's voice echoed up the stairs.

"Check the laundry room!" Rachel called back, giving her wavy hair one last brush.

Rachel slipped on her favorite pair of white beaded dress boots, a concession to her cowgirl heart that somehow worked with the feminine dress. As she descended the stairs, the scent of coffee and Felicia's fresh-baked raspberry muffins filled the air.

"There you are," Missy said, emerging from the laundry room with her cardigan in hand. "We're going to be late if we don't get moving."

"We're fine," Felicia assured them, wrapping still-warm muffins in a cloth napkin.

Rachel gathered her Bible and the notebook she used for sermon notes.

"Ready?" Felicia asked, tucking the wrapped muffins into a basket.

Rachel nodded, and her sisters followed her toward the front door. She stepped out onto the porch first, the wooden boards creaking softly beneath her boots. The morning air was sweet with wildflowers and-

She stopped so abruptly that Felicia bumped into her from behind.

"Rachel, what-" Felicia began, then fell silent.

There, parked in their gravel driveway, was the familiar Gold Star Ranch truck. And sitting on their porch railing, dressed in pressed jeans and a crisp blue button-down shirt, was Conner.

The world seemed to pause for a heartbeat as Rachel took in the sight before her. Conner's blue shirt brought out the color in his eyes, and his dark hair was neatly combed, a far cry from his usual windswept look. But it was his expression that caught her breath, a mixture of nervousness and determination that made her heart flutter.

"What's going on?" Rachel asked.

Conner stood, rubbing the back of his neck in that endearingly familiar gesture. His smile was gentle as he met her eyes. "Like father, like son," he said simply.

Something warm bloomed in Rachel's chest, spreading through her entire body like sunshine. She walked toward him, drawn by the quiet sincerity in his voice.

"You're coming to church with me," she said, unable to keep the smile from her voice.

Conner nodded, his smile growing more confident. "Come on, I'll drive."

Behind them, Rachel heard Felicia's soft intake of breath, but it was Missy who spoke first.

"Well, would you look at that," Missy drawled, though her usual sarcasm was softened by something that sounded suspiciously like approval. "A miracle in the making."

Felicia said nothing, but when Rachel glanced back, she saw tears shining in her younger sister's eyes and a tremulous smile on her face.

Conner opened the passenger door for her, a small gesture that made her heart skip. As they pulled out of the driveway, Rachel glimpsed her sisters watching them go. Felicia dabbing at her eyes with a tissue, while Missy grinned and shook her head.

Rachel watched the familiar landscape roll past, green pastures dotted with wildflowers, old fence posts weathered silver by sun and rain, the occasional cluster of grazing cattle and horses. Everything looked different somehow, touched by the magic of this moment.

As they approached the white-steepled church, Rachel noticed Conner's hands tighten slightly on the steering wheel. She reached over and touched his arm gently.

"You okay?"

He nodded, parking the truck in the graveled lot. "Yeah. It's been a long time."

The sun cast long shadows across the church steps as Rachel and Conner made their way toward the entrance. The white-painted doors stood open in welcome, and the sound of the old piano drifted out, playing softly as church members settled into their pews.

Rachel was acutely aware of the heads turning as they stepped inside. Mrs. Brewster, who always sat in the third row, actually dropped her hymnal. But before any awkwardness could settle, Pastor Sam appeared in the foyer, his weathered face creasing into a warm smile.

"Conner Hart," he said, extending his hand. "Welcome home, son."

Conner shook his hand firmly. "Thank you, Pastor."

"We're glad to have you with us," Pastor Sam said simply, but his eyes held a depth of understanding that made Rachel's throat tight.

"I think I know exactly where my sermon is headed this morning," he said with a smile.

Conner and Rachel found open seats near the middle of the church, and Rachel noticed how Conner didn't hesitate or hang back. He moved with purpose, though she could feel the tension in his arm as they sat down. The familiar scent of wood polish and fresh flowers surrounded them, and sunlight streamed through the stained-glass windows, painting rainbow patterns across the worn hymnals and old church pews.

The piano shifted into the opening notes of "Come Thou Fount," and the congregation rose to sing. Rachel handed Conner a hymnal, their fingers brushing.

His voice, when he joined in, was low and slightly uncertain at first, but grew stronger with each verse:

"Come, Thou Fount of every blessing
Tune my heart to sing Thy grace
Streams of mercy, never ceasing
Call for songs of loudest praise"

The words seemed to fill the small church with something larger than themselves. Rachel felt tears prick at her eyes as the congregation moved into the second verse, Conner's voice steady beside her.

"Here I raise my Ebenezer
Here by Thy great help I've come
And I hope, by Thy good pleasure
Safely to arrive at home"

She caught glimpses of the community's reactions as they sang. Old Tom Wilson nodding approvingly, Martha Jenkins wiping at her eyes with a handkerchief, even stern-faced Betty Cooper managing a smile. But it was the peace settling over Conner's features that made her heart swell.

The music shifted then, the pianist transitioning into the next song. The choir leader, Silvia, stepped forward with her guitar, and the first chords of "Amazing Grace (My Chains Are Gone)" filled the sanctuary.

"Amazing grace, how sweet the sound
That saved a wretch like me
I once was lost, but now I'm found
Was blind, but now I see"

Rachel felt Conner's shoulder brush against hers as the congregation swayed gently with the music. When they reached the contemporary bridge, his voice grew stronger.

"My chains are gone, I've been set free
My God, my Savior has ransomed me
And like a flood, His mercy rains
Unending love, amazing grace"

The words filled every corner of the sanctuary, and Rachel blinked back tears. This wasn't just a hymn anymore, it was a testimony, a prayer, and a promise.

As the last notes faded, Pastor Sam stepped up to the pulpit. His eyes swept across the congregation, settling on Rachel and Conner with a gentle smile.

"Today's scripture comes from Second Corinthians, chapter five, verse seventeen," he began, his voice warm and steady. "'Therefore, if anyone is in Christ, the new creation has come: The old has gone, the new is here!'"

Rachel felt Conner shift beside her, sitting up straighter. She could almost see the words settling into his heart.

"God is in the business of new beginnings," Pastor Sam continued. "Every sunrise brings fresh mercy. Every step toward Him is met with open arms. The beauty of God's grace isn't just that He forgives us, it's that He transforms us."

The sermon unfolded like a conversation, Pastor Sam weaving together scripture and everyday wisdom. He spoke about the courage it takes to change, about the power of choosing faith over fear, love over loneliness. Rachel took notes, though her attention kept drifting to Conner, watching how intently he listened.

"Sometimes," Pastor Sam said, his voice softening, "we think we have to be perfect before we come to God. We think we have to fix everything first, clean ourselves up, become worthy. But that's not how grace works. Grace meets us exactly where we are, in our brokenness, in our questions, in our hope for something more."

A murmur of agreement rippled through the congregation. Rachel saw several heads nodding, heard a few whispered, "Amen's."

"The journey of faith isn't about becoming perfect," Pastor Sam continued. "It's about becoming real. About letting God's love transform us daily."

Pastor Sam's words seemed to hang in the air, resonating with truth. "And sometimes," he said, his voice gentle but firm, "the bravest thing we can do is simply show up. To take that first step, knowing God will meet us there."

Rachel felt rather than saw Conner's hand move toward hers. His fingers found hers on the wooden pew between them, intertwining naturally, as if they'd never been apart. The simple gesture spoke volumes about trust, about hope, about choosing to move forward together.

Pastor Sam opened his Bible again. "In the book of Isaiah, we read: 'Forget the former things; do not dwell on the past. See, I am doing a new thing! Now it springs up; do you not perceive it? I am making a way in the wilderness and streams in the wasteland.'"

The sunlight through the stained-glass windows had shifted, painting new patterns across the wooden floors. Rachel felt anchored by the warmth of Conner's hand in hers.

The service drew to a close with one last song, the piano introducing the gentle melody of "In Christ Alone." The congregation stood, and Rachel felt Conner's hand tighten briefly around hers before letting go to hold the hymnal.

"In Christ alone my hope is found
He is my light, my strength, my song
This Cornerstone, this solid Ground
Firm through the fiercest drought and storm"

Their voices blended with the congregation's, and Rachel noticed how naturally Conner followed the melody now, his confidence growing with each verse. When they reached the final stanza, his voice carried clear and strong:

"No guilt in life, no fear in death
This is the power of Christ in me
From life's first cry to final breath

Jesus commands my destiny"

As the last notes faded into reverent silence, Pastor Sam raised his hands for the benediction. "May the Lord bless you and keep you. May His face shine upon you and be gracious to you. May He turn His face toward you and give you peace. Amen."

"Amen," the congregation echoed, and Rachel heard Conner's voice among them.

The usual post-service bustle began, people gathering their things, children being corralled, the rustle of bulletins and Bibles. But there was an extra current of energy today, and Rachel could feel curious glances being cast their way.

Mrs. Jenkins was the first to approach, her lined face wreathed in a genuine smile. "It's good to see you here, Conner," she said simply, patting his arm before moving on.

Others followed, some with just a nod, others stopping to welcome him home. Through it all, Conner stood steadily beside Rachel, accepting each greeting with quiet grace.

Pastor Sam made his way through the crowd, stopping before them with that same warm smile he'd worn earlier. "Conner," he said, "I hope we'll see you again next Sunday."

"Yes, sir," Conner replied, and Rachel heard the certainty in his voice. "I believe you will."

They made their way slowly toward the doors, stopping occasionally to chat with various members of the congregation. Rachel spotted her sisters waiting by Missy's truck. Felicia still looking emotional, while Missy tried to hide her smile behind studied nonchalance.

The morning air was warmer now as they stepped outside, the summer sun high and bright. Bird song filled the air, and in the distance, church bells from the Methodist church across town began to ring.

"You okay?" Rachel asked as they walked toward his truck.

Conner stopped, turning to face her. The sunlight caught the blue of his eyes, making them seem deeper somehow. "Yeah," he said, then smiled. "Better than okay, actually."

Rachel felt her heart swell at the peace she saw in his expression. "You know," she said carefully, "you surprised many people today."

"Including you?"

She shook her head, smiling. "No. Not me." She reached for his hand, squeeze it gently. "I always knew you had it in you."

Conner's thumb traced small circles on her palm, his touch sending warmth through her entire body. "Day by day, right?"

"Day by day," she agreed softly.

From across the parking lot, they could hear Missy's voice: "If you two lovebirds are done having your moment, some of us are getting hungry!"

Rachel laughed, the sound carrying on the summer breeze. "We should probably go before she starts quoting scripture about the sin of making people wait for Sunday dinner."

Conner grinned, opening the truck door for her. "Can't have that on my conscience."

As they pulled out of the church parking lot, Rachel caught a glimpse of them in the rearview mirror. Conner looking ahead with quiet determination, her own face glowing with something that felt a lot like joy. The future stretched before them like an open road, full of possibility and promise.

"Thank you," Conner said suddenly, his voice soft, but sure. "For being here. For showing me the way."

Rachel reached over and took his hand again, their fingers intertwining naturally. "That's what amazing grace is all about," she said simply.

Chapter 31

Rachel watched the familiar landscape roll past her window, contentment warming her heart after the morning's church service. When Conner drove straight past her driveway, she turned to him with raised eyebrows.

"Conner, you passed my driveway."

"Yeah, I know." His lips curved into a smile that sent a flutter through her stomach.

"Okay... well, where are we going? I kind of thought you could come have dinner with my sisters and me."

"I need to run by the house." Conner said, as he turned down the ranch's driveway. A smile playing on his lips. "I have something else in mind."

The truck rolled to a stop in front of the ranch house. "I'll just be a minute," he said, hopping out before she could respond.

Rachel watched through the windshield as Conner disappeared inside, wondering what he was up to. When he emerged a few minutes later, he carried a picnic basket in one hand and what looked like a quilt tucked under his other arm.

Conner placed the items on the back seat before sliding behind the wheel again. The scent of his cologne mingled with something else—was that chicken?—drifting from the basket?

"What's all this?" Rachel asked, curiosity getting the better of her.

"Patience, dear... patience." Conner's grin widened as he backed the truck up and headed back down the driveway.

Rachel settled back against the seat, watching as he turned onto the narrow dirt road that led to the creek. She glanced at Conner, noting how his fingers tapped an irregular rhythm on the steering wheel—a sure sign he was nervous about something.

As they neared the end of the road, Rachel spotted a familiar vehicle and sat up straighter. "Why is Missy's truck here?"

"Just trust me." Conner parked beside her sister's pickup and cut the engine.

He climbed out and retrieved the basket and quilt before coming around to her door. When he opened it, he offered his hand with an old-fashioned courtesy that made her smile.

Rachel took his hand, letting him help her down from the truck. The air was sweet with wildflowers, and a gentle breeze carried the sound of trickling water from the creek. Conner's hand remained wrapped around hers as they followed the familiar trail.

As they rounded the final bend, the massive oak tree came into view. Beneath its sprawling branches stood Felicia and Missy, both wearing knowing smiles that made Rachel's heart skip a beat.

"It's about time," Missy drawled, her usual sass softened by genuine warmth. "What took you so long?"

Felicia stepped forward, taking the basket from Conner, passing it to Missy. Then she grabbed the quilt, shaking it out with practiced efficiency before spreading it beneath the oak's protective canopy. Rachel watched, bemused, as her sisters worked in perfect synchronization. She joined them on the quilt, pulling out containers of food and setting them on the quilt.

The sisters' chatter filled the air—Missy commenting on the food, Felicia arranging everything just so—while Conner leaned back against the tree trunk, watching it all with quiet satisfaction. The afternoon sun slanted through the branches, creating patterns of light and shadow that danced across the scene.

When everything was arranged, Rachel looked up at Conner, her heart full of affection for the effort he'd put into this surprise. "Come on, let's eat. I'm starved, and this food looks amazing."

Conner pushed away from the tree and walked toward her, taking her hand and gently pulling her up. That's when Rachel noticed her sisters backing away, phones raised. She looked up at Conner questioningly, and the expression that crossed his face made her breath catch. It was filled with such tenderness and certainty that it brought tears to her eyes.

He let go of her hand, and in one fluid motion, dropped to one knee before her. Rachel's heart seemed to stop, then start again in double time.

"Rachel Nolan," he began, his voice steady despite the emotion she could see in his eyes. "Ten years ago, I made the biggest mistake of my life when I walked away from you. But God had other plans. He brought me back home, back to you. And every day since then, He's shown me that second chances are possible when you trust in His timing."

Rachel's hands flew to her mouth as Conner reached into his pocket and pulled out a small, burgundy velvet box. The world seemed to narrow to just this moment, just them, as he opened it to reveal a stunning marquise cut diamond ring that caught the afternoon light.

"I love you, Rachel Nolan," Conner continued, his voice growing husky with emotion. "I love your strength, your faith, your capacity for forgiveness. I love how you can take something broken and help it heal. I love being in your presence. I love that you never gave up on believing in me, even when I didn't believe in myself."

Rachel's legs felt weak, and she sank to her knees in front of him, tears streaming down her face. Her heart was so full she couldn't find her voice, couldn't form words past the emotion tickling in her throat.

"I'm choosing you, Rachel. Every day, for the rest of my life. I want to build a future with you. I want to wake up every morning knowing that God blessed me with a second chance at loving you." Conner's blue eyes glittered with unshed tears as he held out the ring. "Will you marry me?"

Rachel's hands trembled where they covered her mouth, her heart thundering in her chest. She was so overcome with emotion that she couldn't speak, could only stare at him through tear-filled eyes.

A gentle grin tugged at Conner's lips. "Well?"

Rachel lowered her hands, revealing a smile that could have lit up the darkest night. "Yes," she whispered, then louder, "Yes, Conner. Yes!"

The joy that blazed across his face was breathtaking. With shaking hands, he slid the ring onto her finger, then pulled her into his arms. Rachel wrapped her arms around his neck as he held her close, both of them still kneeling beneath the old oak tree.

"I love you," she murmured against his neck, breathing in the familiar scent of him. "I love you so much."

The sound of sniffling reminded them they weren't alone. Rachel looked up to see Felicia dabbing at her eyes with a tissue, while Missy tried to maintain her composure, still filming with her phone.

"Well," Missy said, her voice suspiciously rough, "I guess we can stop pretending we're just here for a picnic now."

Felicia laughed through her tears. "I'm so happy for you two." She tucked her phone away and moved forward to hug them both.

"Come here, you big softie," Rachel called to Missy, who was still trying to maintain her tough exterior. Her younger sister rolled her eyes but joined their group hug, though Rachel noticed she was careful to keep her makeup from smearing.

"The food's getting cold," Missy announced after a moment, her practical nature reasserting itself. "And since Conner went to all this trouble to cook…"

"You cooked all of this?" Rachel asked, turning to him in surprise.

"Well, I had some help from your sisters. Turns out they're pretty good at keeping secrets when they want to."

"I can't believe you all planned this without me knowing," Rachel said, settling onto the quilt beside him. She couldn't stop looking at the ring on her finger, and the way it caught the sunlight filtering through the oak's branches.

"Honey, we've been planning this for the past couple of days," Missy said, passing out plates. "Someone had to make sure it was done right."

"What she means," Felicia interjected gently, "is that we wanted to help make this moment special for both of you."

As they shared the simple meal of fried chicken, potato salad, and fresh biscuits, Rachel felt a deep sense of rightness settle over her. The four of them talked and laughed together, sharing stories and plans, while the creek gurgled nearby and birds called from the oak branches above.

"So," Missy said, helping herself to another biscuit, "have you thought about when you want to have the wedding?"

Rachel exchanged a glance with Conner. "We've been engaged for all of thirty minutes, Missy."

"It's never too early to start planning," her sister insisted. "Besides, you two have waited long enough, don't you think?"

Conner squeezed Rachel's hand. "I'd marry you tomorrow if you wanted."

"The church might need a little more notice than that," Felicia pointed out with a laugh. "Though I'm sure Pastor Sam would make an exception for you two."

Rachel leaned against Conner's shoulder, happiness bubbling up inside her like a spring. "Fall would be nice," she mused. "When the leaves are changing..."

"Fall would be perfect," Conner agreed, pressing a kiss on her temple. "And we could have the reception at the ranch."

"With twinkle lights in the trees," Felicia added dreamily. "So romantic."

"And plenty of good food," Missy chimed in. "None of that fancy stuff nobody actually wants to eat."

Rachel smiled, picturing it all—their families and friends gathered at the ranch, celebrating not just their marriage but God's faithfulness in bringing them back together. The image felt right, like a preview of the life they would build together.

"Speaking of the ranch," Conner said, his voice taking on a more serious tone, "I've been thinking about some ideas for expanding the training program. With you running it, of course," he added, smiling at Rachel.

"Really?" Rachel sat up straighter, her interest piqued.

"I was reading through Dad's old journals," Conner continued. "He had some plans drawn up for adding an indoor arena. It would let us work with more horses year-round, maybe even start some more youth programs."

Rachel's heart swelled at how naturally Conner was embracing both their future and his father's legacy. "Warren would have loved that," she said. "He always talked about wanting to do more community outreach through the ranch."

"I know," Conner replied, his eyes warm with understanding. "And I think it's time we made those dreams reality. Together."

Missy cleared her throat. "Well, on that disgustingly romantic note, I think it's time Felicia, and I headed out." She began gathering the empty containers, shooting them a knowing look. "I imagine you two have some planning to do."

"Thank you both," Rachel said, standing to hug her sisters. "For everything."

"Just remember who helped make this happen when you're picking out bridesmaid dresses," Missy said with a wink.

Felicia hugged them both again. "I'm so happy for you," she whispered, then followed Missy back down the trail, leaving Rachel and Conner alone beneath the oak tree.

As her sisters' voices faded into the distance, Rachel turned back to Conner. He was watching her with such tenderness that it made her heart skip.

"Come here," he said softly, pulling her down to sit beside him on the quilt. Rachel settled against him, her head finding its natural place on his shoulder as his arm wrapped around her.

"I can't believe you planned all this," she said, playing with the ring on her finger. "It's perfect."

"I wanted it to be special," Conner replied, his voice low and sincere. "I wanted to show you I'm all in, Rachel. That I understand what matters now."

She lifted her head to look at him. "You've been showing me that every day, Conner. In the way you've committed to the ranch, the way you came to church this morning, the way you've worked to rebuild trust with everyone around you."

"God's been teaching me a lot about patience and faith," he said, threading his fingers through hers. "About how some things are worth waiting for, worth fighting for."

Rachel smiled, remembering their conversation after church. "Day by day?"

"Day by day," he agreed, then grinned. "I'm looking forward to all our days being together now."

"You know what I thought about during the service this morning?" she asked softly.

"What's that?" His blue eyes were tender as they met hers.

"I thought about how God's timing really is perfect, even when we don't understand it." Her voice wavered slightly with emotion. "Ten years ago, I was so angry and hurt when you left. I couldn't see any purpose in that pain. But now..." She glanced down at the ring sparkling on her finger. "Now I can see how God was working in both our lives, preparing us for this moment."

Conner caught her hand and pressed a kiss to her palm. "I needed to learn some hard lessons before I could be the man you deserved," he admitted. "The man God called me to be."

"And I needed to learn to trust His plan, even when it didn't make sense." Rachel's eyes filled with tears of joy. "To believe that sometimes the longest roads lead us exactly where we're meant to be."

Conner pulled her closer, resting his forehead against hers. "I promise you, Rachel Nolan, that I will spend the rest of my life proving that your trust in me—and in God's plan—wasn't misplaced."

Rachel closed her eyes and offered a silent prayer of gratitude. For second chances and healing hearts. For patient sisters and faithful friends. For the man who had left as a boy and returned, ready to build a life with her.

"I love you," she whispered against Conner's lips.

His answer was a kiss that held all the promise of their tomorrows, sweet and certain. And in that moment, Rachel knew without a doubt that this was just the beginning of their new story—a story of faith, forgiveness, and a love worth waiting for.

The creek's gentle music played on, and somewhere in the distance, a whip-poor-will began its song. Their days ahead would bring wedding plans and ranch decisions, family celebrations, and new challenges. But for now, they simply held each other beneath the old oak tree, their hearts beating in time with God's perfect plan.

Epilogue

The autumn evening wrapped the Gold Star Ranch in a tapestry of amber and gold, as strings of twinkling lights danced through the branches of the ancient trees scattered around the reception area. Rachel Hart—the name still new and wonderful on her lips—stood at the edge of the makeshift dance floor, taking in the sight of her wedding reception. Her ivory lace dress, with its fitted bodice and flowing skirt, caught the golden light of sunset, the delicate beading sparkling like morning dew.

"Mrs. Hart," Conner's voice came from behind her, warm and tender. His arms slipped around her waist, and she leaned back against him, savoring the moment. "Have I told you how beautiful you are?"

Rachel smiled, turning in his arms to face him. "Only about a dozen times in the last hour."

"Well, make it a baker's dozen." His blue eyes sparkled as he took in her appearance again. Her honey-blonde hair fell in soft waves around her shoulders, crowned with a delicate wreath of baby's breath. "I still can't believe you're my wife."

Missy's voice rang out across the reception area. "Alright, everyone! Time for the toasts, and as the younger sister, I claim first rights!"

The guests gathered closer, their laughter and chatter creating a blanket of vibrant sound. The setting sun painted the sky in brilliant shades of orange and pink, while the first stars began to peek through the darkening blue above.

The reception tables were adorned with candles and mason jars filled with miniature autumn colored sunflowers, wheat stalks, and burgundy dahlias.

Missy raised her glass, her usual sass softened by genuine emotion. "To my stubborn, beautiful sister Rachel—who always believed in second chances, even when the rest of us," she shot a pointed look at Conner that made everyone chuckle, "needed some convincing. And to Conner, who proved that sometimes the long way home is the right way after all."

"You know," Missy continued, her voice taking on a more serious tone, "I watched my sister pray for you, Conner, even when she thought we didn't notice. And I watched her hold on to faith when it would have been easier to let go. But that's who Rachel is—she sees the best in people, even when they can't see it in themselves." She raised her glass higher. "So here's to love that stands the test of time, to faith that moves mountains, and to my beautiful sister finally getting her happily ever after."

"To Rachel and Conner!" the guests echoed, glasses raised beneath the twinkling lights.

Felicia stepped forward next, dabbing at her eyes with a tissue. "Rachel," she began softly, "you've always been our rock, the sister who taught us to trust in God's timing even when the path seemed unclear. Watching you and Conner find your way back to each other..." She paused, composing herself. "Well, it's reminded all of us that love, real love, is worth waiting for."

Pastor Sam moved to stand beside the newlyweds, his face creased in a warm smile. "There's a verse in Ecclesiastes that seems particularly fitting tonight," he said, his deep voice carrying across the gathering. "'He has made everything beautiful in its time.' Sometimes God's timing doesn't match our own plans, but His wisdom is perfect. Tonight we celebrate not just a marriage, but a testament to His faithfulness."

Rachel felt Conner's hand tighten around hers as Pastor Sam continued. "I've had the joy of watching this community embrace Conner's return, of seeing Rachel's prayers answered, and of witnessing how God can restore what seems lost. This," he gestured to the celebration around them, "is what grace looks like."

Judd cleared his throat, stepping forward with an uncharacteristic display of emotion. "When Warren Hart was alive," he began gruffly, "he used to tell me that someday his son would come home and make this ranch everything it was meant to be. I didn't believe him then." He looked directly at Conner. "But I believe him now. You've proven yourself, Conner. You and Rachel both—you've shown us all what it means to have faith in something bigger than ourselves."

Rachel felt Conner's breath catch beside her, and she squeezed his hand. She knew how much Judd's approval meant to him, how it represented acceptance from the entire ranch community.

The band began to play softly—the opening notes of "Bless the Broken Road" floating through the evening air. Conner turned to Rachel, extending his hand. "May I have this dance, Mrs. Hart?"

Rachel stepped into his arms as their guests cleared the dance floor. Her dress swirled around her ankles as Conner led her in a slow circle beneath the oak tree's canopy of lights. The lyrics seemed to tell their story—of long roads and lost dreams that somehow led them exactly where they were meant to be.

"Look," Conner whispered, nodding toward the gathering. Rachel followed his gaze to see their entire community watching them with joy and affection. Mrs. Henderson was openly weeping into her handkerchief, while Hank Sterling tried to pretend something hadn't gotten in his eye. The ranch hands stood together, their usual rough demeanor softened by the moment.

"Remember the first time we danced under this tree?" Rachel asked softly, her head resting against Conner's shoulder. "We were seventeen, and you were so nervous you kept stepping on my toes."

Conner's laugh rumbled through his chest. "And now look at us. Though I have to admit, I'm still nervous – just for different reasons."

Rachel lifted her head to meet his eyes. "What do you mean?"

"Nervous about living up to all this," he said quietly. "Being the man you deserve, the man Dad believed I could be, running the ranch the right way..."

"Together," Rachel reminded him, touching his cheek. "We do it all together."

The music shifted, and other couples began joining them on the dance floor. Felicia was laughing as Will twirled her beneath the lights, while Missy allowed Levi to coax her into a dance, though she pretended to be reluctant about it.

As the evening deepened, the stars emerged in full glory above them. The oak trees glowed with hundreds of tiny lights, creating a magical canopy over the celebration. The autumn air carried the scent of barbecue from the buffet tables and the sweetness of the three-tiered wedding cake Felicia had insisted on making herself.

"Hey," Marge Squires called out, her eyes twinkling. "Don't forget to cut that cake before these young'uns start sneaking bits of that frosting!"

Laughter rippled through the crowd as Conner led Rachel to the cake table. The creation was a work of art—three tiers of white buttercream frosted perfection, decorated with cascading autumn leaves made of fondant in shades of burgundy and gold. Tiny sugar flowers that matched Rachel's bouquet adorned each layer.

"Now, son," Marge called out with a mischievous grin, "remember that how you treat this cake sets the tone for your whole marriage!"

"In that case," Conner said, wrapping his hand around Rachel's on the knife, "we'll do this together."

As they cut into the bottom tier, Rachel glimpsed Warren's framed photo on the nearby memory table. She'd insisted on having it there, along with photos of her dad and Conner's mother, Luella. Somehow, their presence made the evening feel complete.

The cake was as delicious as it was beautiful, and soon the reception was in full swing again. Pastor Sam found his way to their table, settling into a chair beside them with a contented smile.

"You know," he said thoughtfully, "there's another verse that comes to mind tonight. 'And now these three remain: faith, hope and love. But the greatest of these is love.' I've watched you two demonstrate all three—faith in God's plan, hope for the future, and a love strong enough to overcome any obstacle."

"We had a good teacher," Rachel replied softly, thinking of all the times Pastor Sam had counseled them, separately and together, over the past months.

Pastor Sam smiled warmly. "The ranch is going to flourish under your care. Warren would be proud of what you're building together here."

As the evening progressed, Conner gently took Rachel's hand. "Want to sneak away for a minute?"

Rachel nodded, understanding in her eyes. Together, they slipped away from the celebration and walked to the ranch house. The sound of music and laughter fading behind them as they walked hand in hand beneath the autumn stars.

They climbed the porch steps together and sat on the porch swing. Conner reached over and grabbed the worn leather journal that Rachel recognized immediately.

"Another of your dad's journal," she said softly.

"I found something in here recently that I wanted to share with you." Conner opened to a marked page, using his phone's flashlight to illuminate the words. "It's dated just a few months before he passed away."

Rachel leaned closer as Conner read: "'Watched Rachel with the new foal today. She has a gift that reminds me of Luella—that same gentle spirit, that same unwavering faith. I pray every day that Conner finds his way home soon, not just to the ranch, but to her. They belong together, those two. God has shown me that much.'"

Tears spilled down Rachel's cheeks as Conner continued, his voice thick with emotion. "He knew, Rachel. Even then, he knew we'd find our way back to each other."

"Now," Conner said, pulling a pen from his pocket, "I thought we could start our own tradition." He flipped to the blank pages at the back of the journal. "Writing down our dreams, our prayers, our hopes for the future—right here alongside Dad's words."

Rachel's heart swelled as she watched him write the date and "Mr. & Mrs. Conner Hart" at the top of the page. "What should we write first?"

"How about this," Conner said, beginning to write: "'Today, under an autumn sky, we begin our life together at the Gold Star Ranch. We pray that God will help us honor the legacy of those who came before us while building something new, a home where love, faith, and second chances will always have a place.'"

Rachel took the pen, adding her own words: "'Where children will learn to ride horses and trust in God's timing. Where broken spirits—both human and equine—can find healing and love.'"

A shooting star streaked across the sky above them, and Rachel caught her breath at the beauty of the moment. Conner wrapped his arms around her from behind, and together they watched its trail fade into the darkness.

"You know what this reminds me of?" Conner murmured against her hair. "That verse from Psalm 33:11—'But the plans of the Lord stand firm forever, the purposes of his heart through all generations.'"

"Our own love story is proof of that," Rachel said, turning in his arms. Her wedding dress caught the starlight, the delicate lace and beading shimmering. "God's plans really do stand firm, even when we can't see the whole picture."

From the direction of the reception, they could hear Missy's voice calling: "Where did those newlyweds disappear to? It's time for the send-off!"

Conner chuckled, closing the journal and tucking it safely away. "Ready to face the crowd again, Mrs. Hart?"

"Always," Rachel smiled, taking his hand. "As long as we're together."

They walked back toward the twinkling lights of the reception, where their guests had gathered with sparklers. The golden light illuminated familiar faces. Judd trying to hide his smile, Felicia wiping away happy tears, Missy pretending to be impatient but failing to hide her joy. The ranch hands stood in a group, sparklers held high, while Pastor Sam beamed at them from beside Minnie.

As they reached the edge of the gathering, someone started singing "Amazing Grace," and others joined in, their voices rising into the night sky. The sound wrapped around Rachel and Conner like a blessing, a reminder of the grace that had brought them to this moment.

Through the tunnel of sparklers, Rachel and Conner made their way to Conner's new truck, now decorated with tin cans and a "Just Married" sign in Felicia's elegant handwriting. The autumn air was filled with cheers, well-wishes, and the singing of their friends and family.

Before helping Rachel into the truck, Conner turned to face their guests one last time. "Thank you all for being part of our story," he said, his voice carrying across the yard. "For believing in us, and for helping us build something beautiful here at the Gold Star Ranch."

Rachel looked out at the faces illuminated by sparkler light—all the people who had played a part in their journey. Her sisters, who had never lost faith in her. Pastor Sam, who had guided them. The ranch employees who were family. The community that had loved them through it all.

"God bless you both!" Pastor Sam called out, raising his hand in benediction. "May your love continue to be a testimony of His faithfulness!"

As Conner helped Rachel into the truck, she caught one last glimpse of her wedding reception. The twinkling lights in the old trees, the barn standing proud against the star-filled sky, her family, and friends. This place, these people, had witnessed their journey from childhood sweethearts to husband and wife.

Conner slid behind the wheel, and before starting the engine, he turned to Rachel. "Ready for our next chapter?"

Rachel reached for his hand, her wedding ring catching the light. "More than ready," she smiled. "Though, you know what they say—the best stories are the ones that never really end."

As they drove away beneath the autumn stars, the sound of celebration fading behind them, Rachel's heart was full of gratitude. For the man beside her, for the love they shared, and for the God who had written their story with such perfect grace.

Their journey hadn't been straight or simple, but like the river that wound through the Gold Star Ranch, it had led them exactly where they were meant to be, together with faith in their hearts and endless possibilities ahead.

Leave A Review